W0038340

Grandpa Ed
Sophie MacDonald
Copyright Sophie MacDonald 2013
Published at Smashwords

This Is a Work of Fiction *involving an incest theme with consenting adults, and produced for adult entertainment only. If you do not agree with an adult incest theme do not read this story.*

All characters are over 18. All names, characters, places and incidents are used fictitiously. Any resemblance to actual events or locales or persons, living or dead, is entirely coincidental.

You MUST be over 18 years old to read this story. If you are under 18 or do not wish to view adult content, you must exit now. <u>Adults Only.</u>

Share your thoughts with us.
Take a moment to tell us how we're doing. Your feedback really matters.

You can reach us by:
Email: <u>*my777books@yahoo.com*</u>

Search for other titles by **Sophie MacDonald.**

Grandpa Ed

PART I

Chapter One: Bingo!

The screen door slammed behind Ethel as she left for her weekly bingo session at the school in town, and while that used to be my opportunity to have a little fun, the presence of our granddaughter Molly was going to put a damper on that for the summer.

At 61 years old, I'm sad to sat that my idea of fun had become watching a dirty movie and jerking off while Ethel was out. That had become my fun, and had become the sum total of my sex life as well. Certainly no brag, just fact, and I didn't think that putting on a porn flick would go over well with Molly.

Having Molly around wasn't all that bad, because she was a cute kid who, after an initial few days of rebellion at being sent to us, had calmed down and become agreeable enough. I knew that at her age I would have been plenty resentful at being sent out here in the middle of nowhere too, so it was hard to fault her there.

Having Molly around was certainly easy on the eyes, I had learned in the week she had been around. Especially compared to my dumpy wife, who had become frigid over the past few years in conjunction with a steep decline in her own personal upkeep and

attractiveness.

Molly, on the other hand, was as cute as could be. A slender girl not much more than 5 feet tall with short light brown hair, it was no wonder that the boys took a liking to her, I mused as I watched her sitting in the chair reading a Danielle Steel paperback. I had sprouted more erections in the last week than I had in the whole last decade.

I walked over to the bookcase that Molly was sitting next to and pretended to look for a book while also getting a closer look at her. Molly was wearing a pink sleeveless blouse and had her free hand up over her head hanging on to the back of the chair.

I was surprised to see that Molly had a little hair under her arm. Not very much, to be sure, just a tiny wisp of light brown hair nestled in the pale hollow of her armpit, but the sight of it triggered an immediate response in me, as my cock stiffened rapidly.

It was then that I realized that Molly's eyes had left her book and were now fixed on me, having caught me in what must have become an extended stare. She had a wry little smile in the corner of my mouth as she observed me observing her.

"Oh - I'm sorry Molly," I said after clearing my throat nervously. "Is that sort of thing back in fashion?" I asked nervously. motioning to her furry armpit.

"What? Oh, no, not really," Molly said as she glanced under her arm and then back up at me. "Just lazy I guess. Didn't mean to gross you out."

"Gross? Oh, not at all dear," I answered, and I noticed Molly's eyes had strayed down below my belt, where it had probably become quite obvious that I had not been grossed out. "Brings me back to my youth when that sort of thing was much more common."

"Back in your old hippie days?" Molly said with a giggle.

"That was a little after my time, I'm afraid, but I did used to enjoy watching," I responded.

"So I see," Molly smirked. "Most guys my age would think it was gross. I'll have to remember to shave tomorrow in case some Prince Charming comes by on his tractor to visit."

"Who knows, maybe some Prince Charming would volunteer to do it for you," I chuckled.

"How about you?"

"Pardon?" I asked, not believing my ears.

"You could do it for me," Molly said. "C'mon, it'll be fun!"

With that Molly threw down her book and jumped up from the chair, grabbing me by the hand and leading me down the hall to her room.

Chapter Two. Molly's bedroom.

My head was spinning as I followed my granddaughter down the hall and into her room, where she turned on the light and started rummaging through her things before emerging with a can of shaving cream and a disposable razor.

"Here you go Grandpa Ed!" Molly said as she handed me the items. "I don't want to get this blouse messy so I'd better take it off."

Molly pulled the blouse over her head and folded it neatly before setting it on the dresser.

"There! I would take this off too," Molly said in reference to the sports bra she was wearing, "but you'd probably make fun of how small my breasts are."

"No," I said, meaning that I didn't want her to take her bra off, but Molly didn't take it that way.

"Okay then, as long as you don't laugh," Molly said as she peeled the bra off before I could say anything. "See how flat chested I am?"

My eyes were drawn to Molly's breasts even though I honestly made an effort to avert my eyes at first. Molly's breasts were indeed small, about the size of lemons cut in half, and the little buds were capped with tiny rose-colored nipples not much bigger than my own.

"There, now I'm comfy!" Molly exclaimed as she fell back onto her bed and put her hands behind her head and waited for me.

"This isn't right," I protested.

"We haven't done anything wrong," Molly said. "C'mon Grandpa. You're bored - I'm bored, so what the hell?"

Bored did not justify what I found myself doing as I knelt beside Molly with the shaving cream can and razor. I was shaking the can mindlessly, although the way my hands were trembling that might not have been neccessary. I squirted out a tiny ball of the foam into my palm and looked at Molly, who seemed amused at my discomfort.

My hand moved toward Molly, and when I dabbed the cream into the little spray of hair and started rubbing it around the fur, Molly let out a little sigh that sounded like pleasure.

Me? I was disgusted with myself, but not disgusted enough to stop my erection from trying to explode through my pants as I massaged the shaving cream into Molly's modest

patch of armpit hair for far longer than was necessary.

After I finished applying the cream, I wiped off my hand on the washcloth I found on the corner of the night table and picked up the razor, trying to figure out how I could make this last longer than the one swipe of the blade that was actually necessary.

With gentle strokes, I slid the razor under Molly's arm a couple of times before pausing to clean the blade and then giving it a final pass. I took the washcloth and wiped the residue from under Molly's arm before inspecting my work.

"There!" I croaked. "Smooth as could be."

"Kissably smooth?" Molly cooed.

Almost as if I was under her spell, I leaned forward and brought my lips to the smooth damp skin, and hearing Molly gasp I found myself sliding my tongue up and down the moist hollow as Molly's whole body shivered.

Molly's eyes were closed and her mouth was open when I pulled my head back from her. On her back, Molly's little breasts had disappeared completely, with only the little nubs of her now-erect nipples disintingushing her sex, and I found this androgynous look incredibly arousing.

"You okay Grandpa Ed?" Molly asked, and I must have looked a sight. Sweat was flowing down my face, which felt flushed as well.

"I'm fine Molly," I said as I rose unsteadily to my feet.

"Here Grandpa, I'll just swing around and you can stay there," Molly said, and she spun around on the bed so that now her feet were at the head of the bed. "Gotta do my other pit, remember? I've got two of them," Molly reminded me with a giggle.

"Right," I said as I knelt down again, pausing to look at Molly's legs, which were slender yet shapely, and I'm ashamed to admit that I was hoping they needed shaving too, but they appeared smooth with the eception of a light golden down on her thighs.

"This is fun, isn't it Grandpa Ed?" Molly said as she watched my squirt some foam into my palm.

"Sure, I guess," I admitted, knowing this was very wrong and feared it had the potential to get ever more so. Very wrong, and very wrong to be enjoying this so much as well.

"Oooh that feels so nice when you do that," Molly said as I rubbed the shaving cream into her other armpit.

I was going to tell Molly that the pleasure was all mine, but was unsure on how she

would take it, and I didn't want to come off as any more of a pervert than I already was.

"So Grandpa Ed," Molly said as the razor mowed down the fuzz under her arm, "I bet you've got a big cock."

I dropped the can of shaving cream in shock, and was fortunate I didn't slice Molly up when I heard her say that, and looked at Molly in horror.

"Molly!" I protested.

"Well, you've been walking around with a boner ever since I got here, and it sure looks big," Molly opined. "Grandma Ethel is a lucky lady, I'll bet. Whatcha got, 7 or 8 inches?"

"That's not an appropriate topic for us to be discussing," I told Molly as I wiped her underarm dry.

"Aren't you going to check to see if this underarm is smooth too?" Molly purred. "Your tongue felt so nice when you licked me that I almost came."

"I think we've gone far enough with this," I told Molly firmly.

"We haven't gone anywhere yet Grandpa," Molly said as she spun around and sat on the bed facing me. "Take it out," Molly said as she grabbed me by the belt and held me in place.

"Molly, please."

"You want me to take it out for you?" Molly cooed before grabbing the bulge in my trousers and stroking it.

I could have easily broken free, but instead stood there frozen as Molly stoked my cock through my pants. My knees were weak and my head was spinning.

"Damn, it feels really big Grandpa. Is it?"

"I don't know Molly."

"Bullshit!" Molly snapped. "All guys know if they're big or not, and yours feels enormous."

"Yes, I'm a little on the large size I guess," I finally admitted.

"Bet you'd like me to get you off right now," Molly said.

"We can't. We just can't."

"Bad time of the month for me, but I can give you head," Molly said. "Want me to suck your dick for you?"

"NO!"

"Please Grandpa, how about if I just jerk you off then?" Molly almost begged. "I'm no innocent kid you know."

Molly took my silence for what it was, which was me wanting her to do whatever she wanted to do to me, so I did not protest when Molly unbuckled my belt and undid my pants. They fell off me with a clunk as my change tinkled out onto the carpet. Molly unbuttoned my shirt and pulled that off me as well. I stepped out of my pants and stood there clad only in my boxers and socks.

"Lay down Grandpa," Molly instructed me, and we changed places on the bed. "You're furry as a bear," Molly exclaimed as she ran her hands through the silver hair that coated my chest and belly.

"Oh man, look at the size of this baby," Molly said as her hand slid over the bulge in my boxer shorts that extended down my thigh. "You like it when I rub it like this?"

"Yes," I croaked weakly.

"Want me to take off your underwear and play with your dick?" Molly asked seductively.

"Please..."

Molly's hands came up to the elastic of my shorts and began to slowly tug them down. I lifted my backside up to make it easier for Molly, who promptly whisked them down to my knees and then right off.

"Oh man!" Molly exclaimed as my manhood came free and sprang back to my stomach. "Your cock is fuckin' huge!"

Molly took my cock my the head and pulled it upright, sliding her hand slowly down the entire length of my cock. I was so hard that the skin was stretched to the limit, and the veins that ran along the shaft seemed to be pulsating.

"Bet Grandma can't get enough of this big boy," Molly said with a grin.

"No - we don't. Haven't in so long," I grunted as I watched a bead of cum ooze out of the tip of my cock.

"You don't fuck her anymore?"

"She doesn't want to," I admitted.

"Does she do this?" Molly asked, and bowed her head over my dick before her tongue swirled around the crown, causing me to moan loudly.

"No," I gasped.

"You want to cum, don't you Grandpa?" Molly said as she got up and grabbed a bottle of baby oil off the night stand, pouring some into her cupped hand.

"I want to watch you cum," Molly said as she rubbed her hands together so they were covered with oil. "I'm gonna milk that big dick dry for you Grandpa."

Molly knelt beside me and took my cock in her fists and began pumping it in a gentle rhythm. I felt the cum begin to rise already inside of me, and I fought to keep control. Molly seemed to sense this and so let go of my cock for a minute and oiled my nut sack.

"Big balls too," Molly said. "Gee Grandpa, you're hung like a horse. Bet you had the girls chasing after you before you got married, didn't you Grandpa?"

"Some," I said as I spread my thighs apart to allow Molly better access to my sack, which she kneaded with enthusiasm.

"Your dick is even bigger than Billy Steele's - he's this dude back home that I dated," Molly informed me. "I want this inside me so bad."

Molly resumed jacking me off, talking dirty to me while bringing me to the brink of orgasm time after time, only to back off at the crucial time. I was drenched in sweat and breathing heavily while I watched Molly's little hands sliding up and down my cock, squeezing the bulbous head at the conclusion of each stroke.

Molly was teasing me expertly, always knowing when I was about to come and then slowing down. She was obviously no innocent kid, just like she had said, and after what had to be ten minutes of this exquisite manipulation, my cock had changed from a pale pink to a hue that was somewhere between crimson and purple.

"Does Grandma go to bingo every Tuesday, Grandpa Ed?" Molly asked, as she brought my hand up to her little titty, and I massaged the bud with my palm, the nipple hard and pointy.

"Yes," I said. "Please... need to cum."

"I know you do, and you will," Molly said. "Next week, I want you to fuck me."

"Can't!" I said. "It's not right."

"Next week," Molly insisted. "Next week I'll let you shave my pits again, because that

really turned me on, just like it did you. Then I want you to fuck me with this gigantic cock of yours. I want all 9 or 10 inches, or however big it is, all of it in me. I want you to split me in two. You know you want to! Say you will. Say you want to fuck me. Say it!"

"Yes!" I groaned. "Please... yes. I want to fuck you. I'll fuck you. Please!"

"Deal!" Molly exclaimed, and she bent down and began bobbing her mouth up and down the head of my cock while her fists pistoned up and down the shaft violently. I let out a guttural scream from somewhere deep in the depraved depths of my soul, and as I howled, Molly's mouth came off of my dick just in time.

I came like I never had before. Cum spurted out of my tortured cock like a geyser, spraying wildly in the air as Molly cackled with delight. After years of watching my best efforts result in a tiny dribble of sperm, watching what was happening was surreal, as thick ropes of cum continued to erupt from me for a scary length of time before finally stopping.

"Holy shit!" Molly said as she looked at the mess she had created. Stringy strands of cum were all over my chest and stomach, and Molly's hands and arms were decorated liberally as well. Molly let go of my withering cock and lifted her arms up to marvel at the semen garland hanging off of them.

"Hope you got some saved up for me next week Grandpa Ed," Molly said as she got up and headed for the bathroom. "I can't wait."

As the cum cooled on my body, I rose and looked at myself and the mess that I had become. I looked everywhere except at my face. Somehow, I had no desire to look at my face in the mirror now.

PART II

Chapter 1. Restless night of frustration.

I could hear the clock in the hallway ticking, and the constant rhythm did not make sleep come any easier. The green glow of the clock radio on the other side of my wife Ethel told me it was 12:06, and it seemed like time was standing still.

My eyes were now accustomed to the darkness after lying here for the last two hours, and my gaze went Ethel's plump shoulder, and the huge breast that rose and fell with her breathing. How long had it been since we had made love? Three years? Four? Too fucking long to keep up this charade of a happy marriage as anything more than a cheap facade.

I reached my hand over and placed it on that big tit, and I squeezed the doughy flesh out

of boredom. My cock began to stiffen despite the lack of desire I had for the woman, and I was just getting interested when Ethel snorted and rolled away from me and onto her side.

Her huge ass was peeking out from over the sheet which had come down to around our knees with all the tossing and turning, and I pulled my cock over while sliding over toward Ethel and the clump of hair sprouting from between those cheeks.

If I fucked her in the ass at least we wouldn't have to look at each other when we did it, I thought to myself as I poked the head of my dick between those fat ass cheeks. Not much chance of that happening, I figured, and after a few timid pokes of my cock produced nothing more than another snort from Ethel, I gave up.

I slipped out of bed as quietly as possible and went down the hall to the bathroom. After tapping the reluctant kidneys I headed out to the kitchen for a drink. At the end of the hall was the spare bedroom where our lovely granddaughter Molly was sleeping, the cute little thing who had turned my world upside down last Tuesday night, and had made me promise an even more interesting time this Tuesday night.

Molly always slept with the door closed, so I was shocked when I noticed the door was ajar when I went past it. I gave a glance inside as I went past and stopped dead in my tracks.

Molly had worked her sheet part of the way off on this humid summer night, and thanks to the light of the full moon that streamed in through the window I could see that Molly slept in the nude. Laying on her side I could see the side of her tiny breast and her pert left buttock.

No, no, no, I told myself as I kept walking after a long look, and went to fetch that drink in the kitchen. How much life had changed since Molly had moved in for the summer. Walking around with constant erections, looking for opportunities to brush up against my granddaughter, and just now actually wanting to fuck my wife. What the hell had Molly done to me?

Chapter 2. Just walk on by.

After getting a drink I wandered back upstairs, and tried not to look into Molly's room, failing miserably. Molly was no longer on her side, for she was now on her back, with arms and legs akimbo, and fully illuminated by that helpful full moon.

I pushed the door open a little bit wider, very thankful that this was one of the few doors in our old farmhouse whose hinges didn't squeak whenever you opened it. Silently I walked over to the side of the bed, the same side where last Tuesday I had been lured into shaving my little Molly's underarms, and she had reciprocated by masturbating me into an orgasm so intense that I still couldn't believe it.

Now here I was again, staring at this precious little woman; Molly's diminutive breasts disappearing with her on her back, those little pointy nipples standing up proudly, and now for the first time my eyes strayed below her waist.

Such beauty, I thought to myself as I gazed at her most intimate area, and without thinking my hand reached inside my pajamas and pulled out my stiffening cock. Molly's legs were spread a bit and her knees were bent, affording me an ideal view of the little tuft of light brown hair that guarded her tender opening. I couldn't have gotten a better view if Molly had been trying to provide me one, but her eyes were closed.

I intended to leave just then, as Molly stirred a bit, but as she did her knees raised up a bit and her thighs parted. The only sound in the room was my breathing, which sounded like a freight train going up an incline.

I found that wasn't walking out of the room - instead I was climbing onto the foot of the bed as gracefully as a man my size could, and crept up to where my head was between Molly's legs. From there, my head slowly bowed until her pussy was so close I could smell the sweet perfume that rose from it.

Then my cheeks were being gently carressed by the softest spray of pubic hair imaginable. Hair so soft it was more like down, and my tongue grazed the silky fur along Molly's labia before letting it slip inside of her.

Molly let out a little gasp, and I knew that she could not still be asleep, or even if she had ever actually been asleep to begin with. No matter, because once I had inhaled the aroma of Molly's sweet pussy. a combination of a vague floral scent with a musky, lusty overtone, I was long past stopping.

My tongue burrowed into Molly, lapping like a madman from top to bottom, and even letting my tongue dart down way between her thighs and licking her anus briefly. It all tasted sweet to me. My God, how long had it been since I had tasted flesh as sweet as Molly's?

My mouth found the shy pearl of her clitoris, and as I swirled my tongue around it, cupping her little ass chheks in my palms and trying to force more of her into my mouth, Molly began writhing and squirming beneath me.

Molly was whimpering and moaning, and I remembered that I had not closed the door behind me when I had entered, but I was way beyond caring by then. When she came, my mouth was drenched by a spray of sweet nectar, and my tongue kept splashing on through it as Molly's thighs clamped around my head while her orgasm raged.

Finally, Molly's thighs released my head as they parted wearily, and I rose up on my knees and looked up at Molly, whose eyes were still closed as if nothing had happened, but whose chest was rising and falling rapidly.

Wordlessly I backed down the foot of the bed, climbing off as inconspiciously as I could manage, and walked silently out of the room, pulling the door closed behind me.

I got back in my own bed and looked over at Ethel, who was sleeping as if nothing had happened. I pulled a sheet over her big butt, which no longer seemed particularly appetizing, and lay on my back. I considered masturbating, as I had gotten so wrapped up in Molly that I had forgotten about myself.

The smell of Molly's pussy permeated the air, as my face was coated with her cum, and I wondered whether it would be that obvious to Ethel if she woke. My hand strayed down to my cock, but after a few half-hearted tugs, I gave it up and closed my eyes, thinking about Tuesday night and what was going to happen.

Chapter 3. What a dream I had.

My dream was so realistic I never wanted to wake up. In my mind, I was putting my cock into Molly, and she was having orgasm after orgasm, and her moistness was gripping my cock as I felt her tight pussy convulse with pleasure.

I awoke with a start, and realized that I must have been snoring, like I occassionally do when I fall asleep on my back. The thing that really startled me was that my dream was continuing even though I was awake.

Molly. I jerked my head to the side and saw the hulking shape of my wife, still sound asleep with her back to me. Kneeling down toward the foot of the bed was Molly, and she had the shaft my cock in her hands and was sucking on the bulb furiously.

What if Ethel woke up and saw her granddaughter doing this? The thought both terrified me and excited me, and as my eyes adjusted to the surroundings I could see Molly looking up at me as she licked and sucked the crown while her hands twisted and jerked the rest of it.

The bed was moving ever so slightly with the motion of Molly's head and hands, and she seemed to be having trouble getting much more than the head of my cock into her petite mouth, but it felt so good that I was not going to complain.

The danger part began to weigh heavily on my mind, so much so that I put my hand down between my legs, underneath Molly's hands, and began rubbing hard on the area between the base of my cock and my balls.

This rarely failed to make me cum fast when I abused myself, and as I felt the cum surge through my loins I could only wonder whether Molly had expected to finish me off in her mouth. The question was moot seconds later as my cock began ejaculating, and my warm seed shot into Molly's mouth.

I felt Molly's tongue swabbing the tip of my dick as I came, so she was not only expecting it, but knew what to do with it when it arrived. I managed to make much less noise that I wanted to, but only by biting my lip and confining my sound to a few stifled snorts.

My cock began to grow limp, but Molly kept sucking, and as it shrunk to a more manageable size, Molly began to demonstrate some incredible cocksucking skills. Soon she had my limp tool all the way in her mouth, and she kept moving his lips up and down me, stretching and sucking it until I had to gently pull her off, longing for the days of my youth when it would have risen again in a matter of minutes from such affection.

Molly crept off the bed and ducked over to give me a kiss with her sticky mouth before whispering in my ear, "You taste yummy Grandpa," and making her way out the door.

"Quit rockin' the boat," Ethel said in a sleepy moan as she rolled over.

As Ethel rolled over, her meaty arm came around and fell across my stomach, her pudgy fingers just inches away from my flaccid cock which lay back on my gut contentedly.

Timing is everything.

PART III

Chapter 1. Get out the door already.

Tuesday night had arrived, and the tension filled the dining room, or at least my corner of it. Ethel was oblivious to it all, of course, and filled the air with inane chatter about some cover-all that she had almost won the week before at bingo.

Molly seemed not a bit nervous either, and kept her grandmother going by peppering her with questions about the stupid game, pretending that she gave a damn about it.

"You should come with me some week Molly," Ethel suggested. "You'd have a lot of fun - we all do. It's mostly us ladies, but there's a few men there too. Some men like to do things with their wives."

Zing! Another barb directed at me by the old bag, who rarely passed on the opportunity to jab at me, this time aimed at my lack of interest in sitting in a school cafeteria with a bunch of old biddies and yelling at an even older geezer to draw their numbers. I had gone once a long time ago to make her happy, and swore that would be the last time.

"Some men must be morons," I muttered under my breath, and passed on the opportunity to repeat myself when prompted to by Ethel.

I didn't want to prolong the agony of waiting by getting into it with Ethel, and only wanted her to get out the door as fast as possible. The clock seemed to be going in slow

motion as well.

Molly was now playing footsie with me under the table, rubbing my calf with her toes, and if she wasn't so short and was able to reach my crotch from across the table, I had no doubt she'd be doing it. I smiled in recognition at her antics and asked Molly to pass the butter.

"What are you two planning on doing?" Ethel asked.

"I dunno. Maybe watch a movie or something," I suggested.

"Well, just remember that there will be someone else in the audience with you when you pick one out," Ethel snorted, and I nodded while resisting the urge to jump up and punch her lights out once and for all.

I was never able to understand why some men get violent with their wives, but after the last few years of being tormented by this dried-up drone I was beginning to realize how some men break under the pressure. Not justifying it, mind you, but just understanding.

Ethel's film jab had been aimed at her finding my porn stash of movies a couple years back. I begged her to watch one with me, in hopes that it would kindle something inside of Ethel - something that had been gone for a long time.

What it kindled was rage, because even though I had selected a tame soft X movie without anything graphic in it, after ten minutes she jumped off the couch and started screaming at me.

"How dare you bring that filth into our home!" I remember her screaming at me, waving that fat ham of an arm wildly as she shrilled on.

"You must be some kind of pervert to spend your money on vile filth like this," she continued. "Then you show how little respect you have for me by insisting I watch it with you. You're going straight to hell Ed, but don't try and drag me down with you!"

Too late for that, I remember saying, because I was already there, but that didn't stop her from going on and on that night. I recall finally tuning her out when she started quoting scripture at me, and I resisted reminding her of some of the crazy stuff we had done in our younger days, back when we were in love.

"Did you hear what I said?" Ethel snapped at me, breaking me out of my daydreaming about the bad not-so-old days.

"Huh? What? Watch out for what movies we watch. Yes dear," I said in my best W.C. Fields imitation, and thinking how I used to find it so funny when it was someone else being henpecked.

"If you had been listening, you would have heard me tell you that I have to drive this week, because Betty's car is in the shop," Ethel apparently repeated.

"Fine," I answered, and knowing what a rotten driver she was gave me reason to hope that she would run into a tree or something. It would be worth sacrificing our new car for such an event.

Molly helped Ethel with the dishes as I busied myself by taking out the trash, all the while counting the minutes until Ethel's departure, and figuring in that she would have to leave a little earlier because she was driving, and would be home a little later. All the better, as it would give me a few more minutes with Molly.

Chapter 2. Ethel's departure.

Finally, Ethel gathered her bingo crap together; her special markers, her lucky charms (including a real horsehoe - I kid you not), her stuffed animals and all the other nonsense and headed out the door. I raised my head up from the newspaper and grunted a goodbye as the door slammed behind her.

I listened for the car engine to start, and heard the crunching sound of the tires backing up through the gravel driveway before jumping up and looking out the window and watching the beautiful sight of Ethel driving down the road.

I raced into the kitchen looking for Molly, and not seeing her there flew up the stairs faster than I had ever done before and headed for Molly's room. There she was, laying on her back as naked as a jaybird, hands behind her head and smiling when I charged in.

"What took you so long Grandpa Ed?" Molly said teasingly as I began unbuttoning my shirt as fast as I could, tossing it over in the corner.

"Thought she would never leave," I muttered as my trousers fell to the floor and I jumped out of them.

"Slow down Grandpa Ed," Molly said. "We've got lots of time. Leave your boxers on for me. I like to take them off myself. Besides, there's something you gotta do first, remember?"

Molly nodded over to the night stand, where the can of shaving cream sat next to a fresh razor, and so I dutifully knelt beside her bed and grabbed the equipment.

"Take your time Grandpa Ed," Molly instructed me. "That really turned me on last week. You liked it too, didn't you?"

"Yes," I managed to croak, as I shook the can and stared at Molly's armpit, noting the tiny patch of fuzz that had grown in the past week, barely visible to the naked eye.

"You ever do this to Grandma Ethel?" Molly asked, and I rolled my eyes at the thought. "That would take you quite a while, because she's really hairy. Reminds me of my best bud Angie. One time we shaved each other all over, and it took me forever."

"You and your friend Angie shaved each other?"

"Yeah, all over," Molly said. "She's so hairy that it took me forever to shave her, especially her bush."

"You mean you shaved each other's..."

"Pussies," Molly said. "You reminded me of her last week when you licked my underarm after you shaved it, just like she did."

"She did? What - why?"

"Well, that's not all she licked," Molly said while making a face. "That bother you, me getting it on with a girl?"

"Well, I don't know. No, I guess not," I said as I pictured Molly and a girl going at it just like in the movies, and I bent over a little bit to adjust my cock which had run out of room in my boxers after listening to Molly.

"Good, because I like it a lot," Molly said. "Maybe Angie can come up and visit me before the summer is over and you could watch us get it on with each other. Maybe you could join in, because Angie has a real thing for big cocks like yours. Me, I like them all, big or small."

Sweat was rolling down my face and down my sides and I squirted some shaving cream in my palm before rubbing it under Molly's arm.

"Mmmmm... that feels so good," Molly said as I massaged the foam into her stubble. "Is your cock hard right now Grandpa Ed?"

"Very," I said softly.

"Oooooh!" Molly said as the razor slid through the faint growth with ease. "I loved it when you came into my room the other night and went down on me. You were so good at it. Almost as good as Angie is."

I tried to say something but could only make a gargling sound as I slid the razor back through for no reason other than the thrill of it, before wiping the residue from her underarm and inspecting my work.

"Smooth Grandpa?" Angie said, and on cue I bent over and raked my tongue up and down the moist hollow, feeling no trace of anything but smooth and softly scented skin,

as Molly shuddered beneath me.

Molly spun herself around so that her feet were on the headboard and I began the meticulous process on the other side.

"Did you like it when I came into your room afterward Sunday night and gave you head?" Molly asked as I tried to see what I was doing despite the sweat flowing down into my eyes.

"Yes."

"I wish I could have done better, but your cock is so big I couldn't even get half of it in my mouth, Molly said.

"It was wonderful," I said as I checked my work with my tongue and got the familiar response from Molly.

"You really want to make love to me, don't you Grandpa Ed?" Molly asked, and I nodded affirmatively in response. "I can tell because I can see how excited you are, and the way you look at me. See how hard my nipples are?"

I reached over and rubbed the little pegs with my fingers, feeling their taut pebbly texture.

"I'm already wet for you Grandpa Ed, want to see?" Molly asked while swiveling around and lifting her leg over my head, leaving me facing Molly's pussy.

The scarity of hair made it easy to see her opening was glistening, and I kissed the tender opening while dipping my tongue inside of Molly, and my licking soon had Molly squealing. Nothing had ever tasted so sweet or smelled as erotic as that delicate valley between my Molly's parted thighs that night.

"Stand up Grandpa Ed," Molly said as she sat upright on the edge up the bed, and I slowly managed to get to my feet.

Molly grabbed my boxers and yanked them down, and my cock celebrated its freedom from being pinned to the inside of my thigh by springing up crazily as it came free, nearly clubbing poor Molly who dodged to get out of its way.

"I'm scared Grandpa," Molly said as she reached over for her baby oil and hosed down my cock and balls with the lotion before working it in with her hands. "I'm really excited but I'm scared too. Guys always say that I have a really tight pussy, and you're so much bigger than they were."

"I'll be gentle baby," I said while stopping Molly from making me cum with her vigorous oiling of me.

"Don't worry if I cry or anything, 'cause I'll be okay after I get used to it," Molly said as she rolled over on her back, putting a pillow under her backside as I climbed up on the bed.

I happened to look over at the mirror on Molly's dresser and saw the scene from a different viewpoint. The tiny teenager with thighs parted in anticipation, and me, at well over 6 foot and over 200 pounds looking like a monster as I knelt there with my throbbing cock glistening and bobbing menacingly in front of me. In shame I admit that the sight was astonishly erotic to me.

I looked down as I rubbed the beet red crown of my cock along the slick lips of Molly's pussy before slipping the tip of it between the sparsely furred lips and pushing forward.

"OW!" Molly howled as I pushed forward hard in an attempt to squeeze the bulbous head of my member into her tiny opening.

Molly's face contorted in a gruesome way as I tried to squeeze inside of her, and I would have stopped if it weren't for the fact that Molly was arching her back to try and help by pushing back. When at last the head of my cock forced its way inside of her with a pop, Molly let out a blood-curdling scream that sounded part pain, part relief and part pleasure.

With the head of my cock now inside her, and feeling like it was caught inside a clamp, I began to slowly rock in and out of Molly, trying to work in a little bit more with every little push.

Molly's eyes were rolling back in her head as she reached blindly over to her night stand where her hand found the bottle of baby oil. She reached down and squirted the stuff liberally all over our crotches, and I began to find it a little easier to penetrate Molly's impossibly tight pussy, what with the lubrication and her body's gradual acceptance of what was inside her.

"Hurts Grandpa," Molly gasped as tears ran down her eyes and down the sides of her face. "Hurts good! God - so big. So fucking big. Is it... all in?"

"Just about, honey," I said after looking down and seeing that I had about half of my cock inside her, if that. "You're really tight baby. You feel so tight - so good."

"Love it - omigod Grandpa!" Molly screamed as her body contorted wildly under me. "Cumming!! OHHHH!!! AAAAAHHHH!!!"

Molly's screams along with her wild trashing had me lose control for a minute, and I thrust myself into her as hard as I could, feeling my nuts slam against her bottom as I rammed myself inside of her with all my fury. This had Molly slamming herself back down onto the mattresss repeatedly while I thrust myself into her without mercy.

My hips were thrusting with the ferocity of someone half my age, and I seemed to have no end to my staying power. Relentlessly my cock drove into her tight tunnel, and Molly came again, her eyes rolling back into her head after her body stopped shaking.

I kept thrusting myself into Molly's tight pussy, and I knew that I could not last as long as I wanted to, because it felt so good. I watched my cock as it went in and out of Molly, and averted my gaze because it was way too stimulating. Looking at her little titties was also too exciting, and when I looked at her face and saw her mouth open with her lips quivering, and only the whites of her eyes showing, I was doomed.

My orgasm soon followed, and the spasming of my cock inside of Molly had her screaming again as my seed squirted inside repeatedly before my orgasm slowly subsided.

I looked down on Molly as I hovered above her, held up by my hands placed next to her shoulders. Droplets of my sweat rained down on Molly's already drenched body, and as my cock deflated inside of her vice-like pussy, our eyes finally met and we smiled.

"Thank you honey," I said. "That was incredible."

"Me too," Molly said, and despite the tears it was clear she had enjoyed it, although she was obviously in a degree of discomfort.

I pulled my flaccid cock out of Molly after a bit, and she gasped when the head popped out and I fell beside her on the bed, both of us looking up at the ceiling.

Chapter 3. Afterward.

Molly and I lay beside each other like that for a few minutes before Molly turned to me and propped herself up on her elbow.

"How long Grandpa Ed?" Molly asked as her hand reached down and grabbed my limp and sticky cock.

"How long?" I asked, wondering what difference that made at this point. It fit inside her, and felt good too, so why ask?

"I mean, how long before you can get it up again?"

"Are you kidding?" I said and exploded with laughter. "Molly, I'm an old man, and I haven't made love in four years. Men my age can't get aroused as often. Not like boys your age."

"I'll bet you that I can get you hard again," Molly said, and reached over me for her old reliable baby oil. "Have to buy some more of this."

The way she had been hosing us down with it, it was no wonder, but as her oiled hands began pulling at my limp noodle, it felt so soothing that I let her go.

"Feels nice anyway, but I'm afraid you're wasting your time," I told her.

"That's okay," Molly said. "I like doing it. Besides, this is the first time I ever saw your cock soft. It's really neat."

Molly held my flaccid pecker upright by the head and chuckled.

"It's bigger soft than most guys are hard," Molly giggled. "You don't mind me saying how big you are all the time do you?"

"There's worse things you could say to a man," I chuckled as I watched Molly pulling on my cock.

"My old boy friend Billy used to love it when I would tell him how big his was," she added.

"It doesn't much matter what size it is if it never leaves your pants," I mused while observing Molly playing with my favorite toy.

"It's so rubbery when it's like this," Molly said as she pulled it out as far as she could. "I never saw one like this before. Seems like it's getting bigger already, at least a little."

"Not going to happen dear, but if you need some more affection I still have a mouth available," I reminded her.

"Only if I can't get you up again, because I can't get over how good you felt inside me, Molly said. "You seemed to like it when I talked dirty to you before, so maybe we can tell each other stories."

"I don't have any stories, I'm afraid," I said apologetically. "I've been stuck in the same boring life for over 35 years."

"You and Ethel never did any swinging or anything like that?" Molly said, and I laughed at that prospect.

"No, I'm afraid that Ethel is not the adventurous type," I asuured Molly.

"Too bad, because I saw pictures of you two when you were young, and Ethel looked like she had a nice body on her," Molly commented. "Big tits too. Guys like that."

"Men like breasts of all shapes and sizes," I told Molly, while looking at hers. Sitting up like she was, her delicate little buds looked irresistable, and I couldn't help leaning

forward and taking Molly's right breast in my mouth.

It was a perfect mouth-sized morsel of a breast, and I sucked on the tiny teat with all the passion within me, and the pointy nipple was rock hard against my tongue.

"Mmmm... that's felt nice," Molly said. "You make me feel like a real woman."

"You are, after all you know."

"I guess, but when I see the way you look at me it makes me feel so warm inside," Molly offered. "Hey, I think you're getting a little harder," Molly said as she flopped my cock from side to side.

"Let's see," Molly said. "You must be a tit man because Ethel had big ones when you married her. My friend Angie is a lot like Ethel was."

"Really?"

"Yeah. Angie has these gigantic tits on her, even though she's like real skinny," Molly exclaimed. "Big ones, just like torpedoes, and she never wears a bra either."

"Is that so?"

"Yeah," Molly said. "Angie's nipples are as big as my whole tits are. She's a Goth chick and is way freaky. Freakier than me by miles."

I tried to picture this Angie girl in my mind, and even though I didn't really know what a Goth chick was, I knew what big tits looked like, and my imagination raced when I thought of the two of these girls making love.

"What's it like making love to another woman?" I asked as innocently as I could.

"It's awesome, because you really know what another woman likes, and it's really magical when it works out," Molly said. "Guys - well, a lot of guys just want to stick it in and that's it."

"And this Angie seduced you?"

"Hell no!" Molly said with a laugh. "My gym teacher at school broke my chick cherry. She used to count heads when we took showers after class, and I guess that she liked what she saw. She didn't really turn me on because she was kinda muscular and really butch, and I was scared of her in a way, but it was still good. After that I was the one doing most of the seducing."

Molly then mentioned that my cock was getting harder, but I had already realized that it gotten to about half mast. I knew it wouldn't last, but let Molly continue to oil my cock

while she kept jerking me off.

"If Angie came to visit me, that would be so far out," Molly said. "When Grandma Ethel would go to play bingo we could all come in her and get crazy. Did you ever fuck anybody in the ass Grandpa?"

"Me? Heavens no."

"Bet Angie would like to take your cock up her ass," Molly said. "She doesn't care how big a guy's cock is. The bigger the better she says. Angie always says that pussies are for eating and asses are for fucking."

"She would want me to do that to her?"

"Do what, Grandpa Ed?" Molly teased.

"You know," I said.

"No, I want you to say it."

"Angie would let me fuck her in the ass?" I asked as my face flushed with embarrassment and the rest of me quivered with excitement. Never did it, even in my younger days, but that didn't mean I wasn't curious.

"Yes, she'd beg you to do it!" Molly said as she jacked me off harder. "I'm getting all hot thinking about watching you stick that fat cock of yours into her ass and making her scream. Angie's ass has a little hair around the hole. Mine doesn't. See?"

Molly turned around and spread her butt cheeks wide, and as I looked at that vulnerable tan puckered ring, I imagined how tight that opening would be.

"Beautiful honey," I said. "It's beautiful."

"What is Grandpa Ed?" Molly prodded me.

"Your anus. Your asshole," I said as she started to correct me.

"You'd like to fuck me in the ass, wouldn't you Grandpa Ed?"

"Yes," I grunted.

"Told you you could get it up again for me!" Molly screamed. "You're as hard as a rock!"

"Won't last," I moaned. "Quick!"

Molly lept astride me, spread her legs wide and lowered herself down onto my cock,

which I held straight up and ready for her descent.

I watched my cock part Molly's pussy lips, and as she slid down onto me she was still incredibly tight, but peneration was easier this time, and I held Molly by the hips while she moved up and down on the top half of my dick.

Molly's face winced as I felt her pussy clamp down around me while she had a little orgasm of sorts, and I had to turn away so I didn't come myself at the sight of this little angel impaled onto my cock.

"Cum Grandpa Ed," Molly pleaded. "I want to you cum! Fast please!"

"Now?"

"Yes, it really hurts. Shoot your cum inside me so it will feel better."

"Alright honey," I said as I looked up at her. "Play with your titties for me honey. Make me cum."

"Like this, Grandpa Ed?" Molly asked and raised her hands up to those delicious little cones, pinching the buds between her thumbs and her index fingers, as the rose colored nipples bulged in response. "You like to watch me play with my boobies?"

"Yes!" I screamed. "Pinch those titties!"

My cock jerked inside of Molly as I came, in what was likely a very small quanitiy of seed this time, but the feeling was incredible nonetheless, and Molly reached down behind herself and jiggled my balls to coax out all she could before collapsing off to the side.

"Sorry," Molly said. "I guess I was more sore than I thought I was."

"It was incredible sweetie," I said as I kissed Molly, our tongues dueling as we embraced.

"You're the best, Grandpa Ed," Molly said. "You're the best man I ever had. Now just think about how much fun we could have with Angie here too!"

PART IV

Chapter 1. Sleep won't come.

It was Monday night as I stared at the green numbers on the clock radio, and I couldn't sleep. Again. 11:59 read the clock visible over his wife Ethel's plump shoulder, 11:59 and holding. How long was a minute allowed to last anyway, I wondered?

Finally - mercifully, the clock blinked and 11:59 became 12:00 and it was no longer Monday. Tuesday had started, and none too soon as far as I was concerned. My cock twitched nervously in my pajamas, almost as if it had learned to tell time and realized what day it was, and what Tuesday meant, and I let my mind take me back in time.

Tuesday was bingo night, and while my wife Ethel went out and played bingo with the other village idiots, I had the opportunity to play a little game of my own with Molly. A game that I thought I would never get to play with another woman again.

How good was it? When I finally managed to cram my cock into Molly's sweet and impossibly tight pussy, it was like I was born again. Never before had I experienced such a feeling, and now that I had enjoyed fucking Molly, I wanted to do it again.

The week now just passed had been torture for me while I had to be around Molly so much. I stared at Molly as she read, as she ate and as she did the dishes. I gawked openly the night last week when we were all watching television in the living room and Ethel had fallen asleep.

As the old crow snored away, I stared at Molly curled up in the chair in the corner, and when she saw me looking at her, she lifted a leg up over the arm of the chair. I looked up under the robe she was wearing, and as Molly lifted it up I could see that she was naked underneath, and that beautiful pussy was staring right back at me, the soft dusting of light brown hair twinkling and glistening.

I motioned for Molly to go out to the kitchen, and I tiptoed out and waited for her. It seemed like forever until she joined me, and when she came out with a mischievious grin on her face, I grabbed her and kissed her hard as I pressed her back into the refrigerator, my tongue finding hers as my cock surged.

"Grandpa Ed, easy," Molly said softly as my hand went into her robe and found her pussy, my finger probing into the moistness. "My pussy is still sore from the other night."

"I want you so bad," I rasped into her ear as my heart began to race.

"I know Grandpa," Molly said as she pulled my finger out of her. "I want you too, but I'm really sore down there."

"You're all I think about," I said as I looked into those doe-like brown eyes.

"I know you do Grandpa," Molly said, and I let out a loud involuntary gasp as Molly's hand reached down and rubbed the bulge in my trousers which was snaking down my thigh. "It's just that you're so very big and my pussy is so tight, that it really hurt."

"I'm sorry Molly," I groaned as my erection throbbed under Molly's stroking. "I tried to be gentle."

"It wasn't your fault Grandpa Ed," Molly said. "I'm just not used to anything that big inside me."

"Please... can't we..."

"I'm sorry, I just hope it will stop hurting before next Tuesday night," Molly said, and I groaned at the prospect of not only waiting until then, but the chance that we might night be able to do it at all.

"What about - the other way?" I asked.

"You mean like this, with my hand?" Molly said as she ran her hand harder on my bulge.

"No."

"You mean with my mouth?" Molly asked coyly, running her tongue over her lips seductively.

"No," I groaned. "Remember when you showed me the other."

"What other?"

"You know, when you bent over and... you know," I said pleadingly.

"Say it Grandpa Ed," Molly demanded. "Tell me what you mean!"

"Your asshole!" I hissed. "Let me fuck you in the ass."

"Grandpa!" Molly gasped. "I could never do that with you. Imagine what your big cock would do to my little bottom. My friend Angie, now she's another story. I told you she would do that. She'd have to come visit me though."

"Fine - call her," I muttered.

"She's one of the kids I was sent here to get away from," Molly said. "You'll have to talk to Grandma."

"I will," I pleaded, now pushing myself into Molly's hand. "Please!"

"Okay Grandpa," Molly said as she reached down and pulled my zipper down, snaking her hand down inside my boxers and yanking on my cock hard.

"Arrrghhhh!" I groaned as I felt my cock jerk in Molly's hand as I ejaculated in my pants, and it was as good as I could have hoped for, standing in the kitchen sweating like a pig while the cum oozed out of me and down my leg.

Molly pulled her hand out of my pants and held it up, showing me a stringy strand of my cum on the back of her fingers. Molly smiled and licked the cum off her hand before winking at me and heading out of the kitchen.

"Where did everybody go?" I heard Ethel ask Molly, having apparently arose from her nap.

"In the kitchen, Grandma," I heard Molly say. "Helping Grandpa. I don't think he feels good."

"What the world is wrong with him now?" I heard the droning voice say in an increasing volume that could only mean she was coming out to the kitchen.

I hastily zipped up my fly just in time, as Ethel barged out to investigate, seeing me leaning against the cabinets.

"What's wrong with you?" Ethel said. "You look horrible. You coming down with something?"

"Maybe," I said, realizing that I must look like that.

"Lord, don't tell me you're going to be needing diapers now!" Ethel said in disgust while gesturing at my crotch, and when I looked down I saw the massive wet stain that reached almost down to my knee.

"Going to bed," I muttered as I staggered past her and out of the room. "I'm sick."

"Well, just make sure you clean yourself off before you get into my bed!"

Chapter 2. Still awake.

12:33 read the clock now, and while my trip down recent memory lane had been enjoyable, it had not sent me off to dreamland as I had hoped. Instead, I had an erection that seemed to be pulsating under the sheet and in no hurry to go away.

I rolled off of the bed and padded out of our bedroom and down the hall to Molly's room. The door was closed as was usual, and I found myself reaching for the doorknob and slowly opening the door.

There was a little night light on, and I could see Molly sleeping, the sheet pulled up to her neck. A considerate grandfather would have tiptoed out of the room and gone back to bed. Well, a considerate grandfather wouldn't have been in the room to begin with, I thought, much less been thinking of perverted things he could do to her.

I pulled the sheet down as subtly as I could, and Molly was naked underneath. My eyes

devoured the sight of my little slut, now looking so innocent as she slept. I wanted to wake her, but decided against it, so instead I coaxed my pajamas down and reached over to her night table, finding her bottle of baby oil.

Squeezing out a handful, I rubbed it on my erection and began sliding my clenched hand up and down the shaft while I stared at Molly. She was on her back, and as my eyes devoured the sight of her little nipples. I tried to decide which I liked better; Molly sitting up with her perky little cones a perfect mouthful, or laying on her back, with all evidence of her breasts gone.

I thought I liked this better, as it gave her a real androgynous look that I found erotic looking, aand while my fist pumped harder I pictured what it looked like when Molly's friend Angie was with her; touching her, sucking on those little buds, parting those tender thighs and tasting her treasure.

Had to work on Ethel tomorrow about letting Molly invite this Angie up for a week, I thought while I neared orgasm. What a sight that would be - seeing this girl and Molly going down on each other.

My orgasm erupted, and I quickly reached down with my other hand and tried to catch the cum as it squirted out, while stifling my grunts of pleasure as best I could. I stood there for a minute with my shriveling cock in one hand and a pool of cum in the other, before pulling my pajamas back up and leaving the room.

In the bathroom, I looked in disgust at my hand which was full of my seed, and held it under the faucet until it all went down the drain. Much more fun to unload it into Molly's pussy, I thought, and thought about other places I could leave it as I went back to my own bed.

Chapter 3. Tuesday night tragedy.

Ethel left and I raced up the stairs to see Molly, but instead of Molly laying on her back waiting for me, she was dressed and reading as I charged in.

"What's the matter honey?" I asked Molly, who put down the book and smiled.

"I'm sorry Grandpa, but my pussy is still sore," Molly said making a face.

"Are you sure?" I whined.

"It even hurt when I put my finger inside of me last night," Molly said. "You know, after you came in and jerked off while you looked at me."

"You were awake?" I said chagrined.

"I'm a light sleeper, and I think that the squishing noise your hand made when you

pumped your cock woke me up," Molly said impishly. "It made me all excited listening to you, so I had to get myself off after you left. Don't be sad Grandpa Ed. We can still do other stuff."

"I guess," I said, ashamed to be sounding like a pouting little brat.

"Don't be sad Grandpa," Molly said as she swung off the bed. "We can still do other stuff."

Molly reached up and undid my trousers and yanked down my boxers, and her eager hands grabbed my flaccid dick and began pulling on it hard.

"I like it when it starts out soft and I get to make it big and hard," Molly said. "It makes me feel like I really did something. Let's get you undressed so you can relax.

I did as I was told, and after I got naked I climbed in bed on my back, and Molly's hands were wrapped around my member in a matter of seconds.

"I got an idea," Molly said. "Would you let me do something to you?"

"What?"

"It's like something you've done to me."

"In that case, go right ahead," I offered, wondering how bad that could be.

Chapter 4. Molly turns the tables.

When Molly returned to the bedroom, she had a package of disposable razors and shaving room, along with a little bowl of water. I smiled as Molly set them on the night table and began taking her clothes off.

"I almost forgot that I hadn't shaved you yet," I said and I began to get up off the bed.

"No Grandpa, you stay right where you are," Molly said."I'm going to shave you!"

"What?"

"Grandpa Ed, you're a hairy bear and I love you, but I want to shave some of the hair around the base of your dick. Won't that be fun?"

"Gee Molly, I don't know about this," I said with concern in my voice.

"C'mon Grandpa, I wanna do it," Molly said. "You have got a lotta hair on the bottom of your dick too, and think shaving it would make it look even bigger than it does now."

"Well, be careful," I said, not at all ceratin about this but wanting to keep Molly happy.

I watched Molly wet the area around my member, which was limp as a noodle by now, and enjoyed the soothing coolness of the shaving cream as she lathered up the entire area. Molly reached down and grabbed the bulb of my penis and stretched it up high.

"It would easier if you had a boner Grandpa," Molly commented, and as I felt the blade glide along the underside of my tool and felt the surge go through my genitals, I knew that would be taking place really soon.

"Wow!" Molly said as she dunked the razor in the water. "Look at all the hair you had down there, and you're hard now too!"

I got even harder as Molly yanked my member from side to side as she shaved me. When I felt the razor begin to go over my balls, I wondered where this would end.

"Need a new razor," Molly said as she unwrapped a fresh one.

"You are leaving a little, aren't you?" I asked.

"Sure Grandpa," Molly said. "Now get up on all fours so I can finish here."

As usual I did what Molly asked, and felt Molly shave the underside of my scrotum very delicately, and then spread my butt crack open and swiped the razor down each side of the crevice before announcing she was done.

"See how cool you look now Grandpa Ed," Molly declared as she shoved a hand held mirror at me.

When I looked down, I had to admit I was shocked. The base of my instrument was pink and smooth as were my balls. The difference in appearance was quite disturbing, as my cock now stuck way out without being partly hidden by my wild silver bush.

"It looks beautiful!" Molly said as she grabbed my cock and stroked it, admiring the smoothness around it.

"Please make me cum," I asked Molly, as my balls were aching and needed release.

"First you have to shave me!"

"Fine!" I said as I jumped up and let Molly take my place while I dug through the bag for a freah razor.

"Not my armpits, Grandpa Ed," Molly said abruptly, and stopped me as I was getting ready to lather her underarms. "I think I'm going to let my pits get hairy for awhile."

"Well, what do you want me to do?" I asked confused, and as I looked at the fuzzy hollows under Molly's arms, realized that for her to become anything resembling hairy would take quite a long time and some doing, seeing as you could easily count the number of little hairs with no problem.

"I want you to shave my pussy!" Molly announced.

"Really?" I asked, looking down at that sparse wisp of ash brown hair that grew around her opening. I was quite fond of that petite bush, and admired the silky softness of the down on my cheeks when I would go down on her.

"Yeah, I'd like you to do that," Molly said.

I nodded and applied a little foam to the soft fur that grew around Molly's pussy and then asked her to swing her legs over my shoulders so I could get a closer look at what I was doing.

I tenderly slid the razor down the outer edges of her little bush and worked toward her labia, pulling the tiny lips up so that I could smooth the entire area. Sweat was rolling down my face as I did some intimate gardening, and I let my thumb apply pressure around Molly's clit every chance I could.

"Oooh."

"What's wrong honey?" I said as I kept playing around the area despite it being as smooth as silk, lifting her buttocks up and inspecting the hairless area between her pussy and her anus.

Molly's anus. It kept drawing me to it like a magnet, even though I had never had any interest in that area before now. So vulnerable looking it was, the tiny puckered ring a ruddy beige hue. I let my tongue slide down the lips of Molly's pussy and below, into the sensitive area between the two orifices.

"Grandpa Ed, did you finish shaving me?" Molly asked.

"Uh - yes Molly," I answered, coming out of the trance I had been in, and Molly swung her legs back around and grabbed the mirror to inspect herself.

"Oh wow!" Molly said gleefully. "My pussy looks so neat, doesn't it Grandpa Ed?"

"It always looked beautiful to me Molly," I said truthfully, although the sight of the bald mound was not unappealing at all.

"Oh gee! You're just saying that because you're my grandfather," Molly said.

My head went down to check my work, and my tongue dipped into the slick opening,

while the soft and smooth feeling of the hairless mound on my cheeks made my cock tingle.

"Can we?" I asked hopefully, thinking perhaps that my groping and licking had made her horny enough to let me put in her. "I won't put it all the way inside of you, honey."

I stood up, and as Molly looked at my cock swaying in front of me, as swollen and crimson as it ever could be, I could see the fear in here eyes.

"Next week, okay Grandpa?" Molly said, and it struck me that the shaving around it certainly didn't help in the decision. "We can do other stuff. Here, climb up between my legs."

I did what Molly asked as she put a pillow under her buttocks and I knelt between her upraised thighs, and I idly began running the head of my tool up and down the channel.

"Ooooh Grandpa," Molly cooed. "That feels nice."

Molly reached down and spread her hairless pussy open, allowing me to rub the crown of my dick around her clitoris, and she began wiggling her hips as I did.

"Oh!" I moaned as I looked down and saw my cock head teasing and probing just inside Molly's little opening. The feeling was very pleasant, but the urge to just slip it in was still there, and I fought it as best I could.

"Harder Grandpa! Rub your dick around there harder!" Molly urged, and my hand began shaking my cock faster along her pussy, as fast as I could do it, swirling the tip around and around her exposed clit as Molly's hands stretched it as wide as she could.

I looked down at Molly's hips twitching... shaking... trying to get off, and her face was beet red and every muscle and vein in her neck was bulging as she cried out... "CUMMING!"

My eyes happened to be looking down between Molly's legs, watching the crown of my dick abuse her tender clit as if it were a little punching bag when I saw it. A little spurt of fluid gushing out of Molly, splashing over my cock as Molly's entire body made a series of convulsions.

Helpless, I felt my cock erupt, belching thick spurts of cum all over Molly. Spraying over her freshly shaved mound, up onto her tummy and then blending with her own fluids inside her pussy. I pulled savagely on my cock, urging a few last jets of seed into the sloppy crevice, and watched the fluid trickle through Molly's pussy and between her legs, down to the bedding below.

"Oh Grandpa, that was so wonderful!" Molly practically screamed her my face and she reached up and hugged me. "I could feel you shooting your load into my pussy when I

was cumming!"

"It was wonderful sweetie," I answered, and it had been. We had managed to have fun despite everything, and Molly promised that next week would be even better.

"Next week we can make love again," Molly promised, and as long as we were careful we could do it a lot.

Being careful when my cock was clamped inside that vice-like pussy was easier said than done, I feared, but I had to try.

Chapter 5. Night dreams.

Later that week, I had a dream. This dream was about Molly, but that was nothing new, since she dominated my thoughts virtually every waking hour as well.

This dream had Molly and I making love, and as I thrust inside of her, she asked me to please stop, as it was hurting her. I told her I would, but only if she let me finish in her ass. She cried and told me that it would hurt even more there, but I wouldn't listen.

I threw Molly on her stomach, and forced my lubricated cock inside that tender opening. I pushed as I hard as I could, despite Molly crying and pleading for me to stop, until the crown of my cock ripped inside of her, and I sank my weapon into her all the way. Molly was crying - screaming - begging me to stop.

But I could not, or I would not stop, and I thrust myself into her ass with a savageness that was almost inhuman. I felt her tender insides tearing under my relentless onslaught, but I was beyond caring, and after I orgasmed into her rectum I pulled myself out and looked down indifferently at the damage I had inflicted on that helpless girl.

I jumped upright in bed like a shot, and looked around to get my bearings. I was in my bedroom, with my wife, and my pajama bottoms were loaded with what appeared to be a copious amount of cum.

Was it real? Had I sleepwalked or something? I bounded out of bed, tears running down my cheeks and headed for Molly's room. I opened the door with a lurch, and must have made quite an entrance because Molly's head came up off the pillow, where she had been sleeping soundly.

"Grandpa?" Molly said groggily. "What's wrong?"

"Nothing baby," I said as I bent down and kissed her forehead. "Just a dream honey. Go back to bed."

I exited the room as quietly as I could and closed the door behind me, leaning against the wall in the hall as I tried to get my heart to beat properly and dried my cheeks.

Dreams about hurting the most precious thing in the world. Having wet dreams as I neared my 62nd birthday. Thinking about having sex with my granddaughter and her friends. Good grief! Molly had arrived in June, and I don't even remember May any more.

PART V

Chapter 1. Behind the barn.

I brought the wheelbarrow full of stones out from behind the barn to the side of the house, where my wife Ethel was using them for the border of a flower bed. When I got there with the stones, Ethel stood up, wiped her brow and tells me that she's going in to lie down.

"Whew!" Ethel brayed. "The heat's taking a lot out of me. Just leave the stones there and I'll finish it later. I'm going to take a nap."

"Fine," I said while watching her waddle into the house and thus giving me a break from being her pack horse, so I went back behind the barn to straighten up the mess I had left behind.

As soon as I got back there, I felt the urge to pee. This was typical these days with me, but I would be damned if I was going all the way back inside to do it, so I stepped back away from the barn and near what I affectionately call my pissing tree and unzipped my work pants.

"Hi Grandpa!" What are you doing?" I heard Molly chirp happily, having just come from around the corner of the barn just in time to see me fidling around in my pants. "Grandpa, are you playing with yourself?"

"No dear," I said as I turned away and put everything back in place. "I just have to relieve myself.

"Huh? Oh, you mean you have to pee?" Molly asked. "I wanna watch! I never saw a man do that before."

"Molly, that's not the kind of thing..." I started to explain, but Molly was already by my side, hanging on my shoulder and waiting.

"You gotta take your thing out Grandpa," Molly explained to me with a giggle, and I rolled my eyes at her before reluctantly reaching back inside my trousers and pulling out my member.

"Yeah! My favorite toy!" Molly cheered as my tool came into view, and I had to chuckle

"Well, I had just gotten out of the shower and went into my room, and Grandma Ethel came in to put some sheets in that spare closet," Molly explained. "I didn't bother covering up or anything, 'cause we're both girls. She asked me if I check my breasts for lumps, and when I told her no, she came over to me and showed me how."

"What the hell," I muttered, picturing Ethel groping Molly's little titties like some old bull dyke. Besides, Molly's breasts were so small that if there was anything wrong it would be easy to see, and I would have noticed myself.

"Yeah, it was real educational," Molly went on. "She felt all around my boobies, and checked my nipples, and felt under my arms too. Then she took her top off and wanted me to help examine her so I knew what to do. Boy, Ethel's breasts are really big, aren't they Grandpa? They're as big as my friend Angie's are, except Angie's are really firm."

"Grandma Ethel's nipples are big too, and then she had me check for lumps under her arms," Molly went on, and I leaned against the tree as the surge roared through my groin. "You should shave Grandma Ethel's armpits like you do mine, because hers are really hairy. They're hairier than yours are, Grandpa."

My knees buckled as jets of my seed spurted out onto the ground, and Molly pumped and milked me with all of her might until I pulled her hand off.

"Wow, that was fun," Molly said as she looked at the back of her hand and licked the string of semen from her knuckles. "We'll have some more fun tomorrow night Grandpa. You know what tomorrow night is? BINGO!" she squealed as she ran around the barn and back to the house.

Chapter 2. Midnight conversations with... Ethel!

That night I woke up for one of my runs to the bathroom, and avoided Molly's room like the plague, needing to save my energy up for later on. When I returned to bed Ethel rolled out and went herself, and when she came back she was in the mood for talk.

"Are you awake, Ed?" Ethel asked, and I grunted a response that I hoped she would take as a no, but I was wrong.

"I need to talk to you about Molly," Ethel said, and my heart skipped several beats.

"What about Molly?" I asked groggily, realizing after a moment that if she had found out, or even suspected what was going on, she would have been screaming instead of whispering.

"I think we should take her to the doctor and have her looked at," Ethel announced. "I think there's something wrong with her."

"Nothing wrong with her," I grunted. "She's a healthy young woman."

"Well, I happened to see her while she was getting dressed, and I couldn't believe my eyes!" Ethel said.

"Oh that's right," I said. "Molly said something about you two checking each other for lumps or something."

"She did?" Ethel asked in a shocked voice, before rambling onward. "Well, the girl has no bosom! She's as flat as a boy!"

"So what?" I said while rolling away from Ethel. "Breasts come in all sizes."

"It's just not right," Ethel said. "There's something wrong with the child. What man would want to be with a girl built like that?"

I was tempted to tell the old battle axe exactly what kind of a man would want to be with a girl like that, but I bit my tongue as she babbled on.

"If you feel like that, then say something to Renee or Todd," I suggested. "It's her parents' business, not yours. Besides, I'm sure she goes to the doctor every year."

"It's just not right," Etel sniffed. "It's not fair that the girl has to go through life looking like that, because she's so cute otherwise."

Eventually I tuned Ethel out and was able to fall asleep, resisting the urge to tell the old crow what I thought of her opinions. Better to get some rest and save my energy for later.

Chapter 3. Molly gets the good word.

"Ed told me you wanted your friend Angie to come visit you for a few days," Ethel said to Molly as we ate dinner Tuesday night. "I wasn't sure about that, but you've been such a good girl so far this summer that I've decided she could come up for the weekend."

"That's really great, Grandma Ethel!" Molly chirped. "Thank you so much, both of you."

I nodded as I tried to picture this girl in my mind while I toyed with my mashed potatoes, and squirmed with anticipation at the thought of what we would be doing.

Ethel eventually left for bingo, and I hopped up the stairs to Molly's room. Molly jumped into my arms the minute I entered the room, hugging me and kissing me wildly.

"Oh, this is going to be so great, Grandpa Ed," Molly exclaimed.

As we were celebrating, and my cock began to stiffen in my trousers, it just occurred to me that Ethel had told Molly to invite Angie this weekend.

"Wait!, I cautioned Molly. "This weekend is no good. Ethel will be around all weekend!"

"Oh poop!" Molly said.

"Wait a minute," I decided while calling an audible. "We'll tell Ethel that she couldn't come up until Monday. Make up something - anything. Better to beg forgiveness than ask permission. Remember that in the future."

"Okay Grandpa Ed!" Molly chirped while running out the door and down the hall. "We can call Angie and tell her."

"What about... you know - us?" I yelled down to Molly, who soon came back up with the phone receiver in hand.

"We can do both at once," Molly said with a smile.

Chapter 4. Phone sex, sort of.

Moments later, Molly and I were both stark naked. Molly was on her back with those shapely and petite legs spread wide, while I had my head between those soft thighs, lapping away at that sweet pussy while Molly called Angie.

"Ang? Molly!" she yelled into the phone, and it was a good thing she was loud because my ears were blocked at the time, and that gave me the opportunity to hear half of an interesting conversation.

"Guess what I'm doing?" Molly began. "I'm getting my pussy eaten, and you wanna know who's doing it? MY GRANDPA ED!"

Nothing like the stark honesty of youth to bring home exactly what I was doing to the light of day, I thought to myself. Strangely enough, it shocked me but did not disturb me greatly, and it did not affect my tongue spinning around Molly's clit, or deter me from having my nose inside her as well, inhaling the sweet scent of her sex.

"Yeah!" Molly continued. "Grandpa is so cool! He shaved my pussy last week. Is it still smooth Grandpa?"

I grunted an affirmative response, as my cheeks felt nothing but smooth skin around her raised mound.

"You gotta come up and visit me Angie," Molly proclaimed,. "Come up next Monday and stay a couple days with me. You gotta let my Grandpa fuck you. I told him you would let him fuck you in the ass. He's HUGE! Oh man!" Molly screamed as she began to cum, and my nose and mouth got squirted while she squirmed on the bed and howled into the phone.

"Oh... wait...I'm back," Molly said panting as she started talking again. "Yeah - I just came. Grandpa eats pussy as good as you do. Now I think he wants to fuck me, that right Grandpa Ed?"

Apparently Molly must have gotten that impression because I had gotten up on my knees, my throbbing erection no longer content with grinding into the bedding, and wanted in. I whispered to Molly to hang up, but she smiled and shook her head.

"Grandpa's gonna put his cock inside me now," Molly revealed. "You wanna stay on the line? Thought so."

I shook my head but began rubbing the crown of my cock up and down her slippery slit anyway, teasing both of us while Molly babbled on the phone.

"Oh - the tip of it is inside me now. Oooooh, the head - Oh!" Molly yelped as the bulb penetrated her. "Easy Grandpa Ed. That's nice. Be gentle Grandpa. He fucked me so good a couple weeks ago, but it hurt me inside, even though I wanted it. Yes, I told you he's big. Way bigger than Billy. Ow, it hurts but it hurts good. Got most of it in. What? Okay, here!"

Molly reached up and tried to hand me the phone, but I couldn't hold myself up with one hand with my other fist wrapped around the shaft of my cock, so Molly jammed it into my neck, where I held it in place with my head.

"Uh, hello?" I asked.

"Grandpa, what the hell are you doing to that little girl?" a sassy voice screamed into my ear. "Got your cock in that sweet pussy huh?"

"Yes."

"Bet that's a tight little snatch for you if you're as big as Molly says," Angie snapped.

"Tight," I grunted while looking down at Molly who was thrusting her hips up to meet mine.

"You oughta fuck her in the ass," Angie said. "She let you do that yet?"

"No."

"Chicken shit little twat," Angie snapped. "What a baby. I'll let you fuck me in the ass next week. I'll bet you like it that way, don't ya?"

"Don't know - never," I managed.

"Tough to talk and fuck at the same time Grandpa?" Angie asked. "Put Molly back on."

I montioned for Molly to take the phone, and she obliged.

"Getting good Angie," Molly said. Here - listen."

Molly set the phone on the bed next to her and began making loud noises, screaming at me with vulgarities meant for the phone audience, and while the phone bill might be tough to explain, I was beyond caring at that point.

I rolled Molly over and stuck it in from behind, a position we both liked because I was able to penerate her even deeper. Molly was chirping away as I thrust into her, and I was grunting loudly as well, the thought of being listened to stimulating me as well.

When we came a few minutes later, my sweaty body crouched over Molly's as my seed erupted into her, we were both screaming at the top of our lungs.

In a minute Molly picked the phone back up, and I fell off to her side as she told Angie how good it was. Molly then handed me the phone once more.

"Hey Grandpa, that was insane," Angie hooted into my ear. "I practically had my fist up my cunt when you two were cumming. Damn, I can't wait to get up there next week!"

"Uh - look forward to seeing you," I offered in response, not knowing what else to say to that.

"Better save up your energy Grandpa," Angie said. "I'm a little tougher to please than Molly. Think you're gonna be up to it?"

"I... hope so."

As I gave the phone back to Molly, who wrapped up the arrangements with Angie, I wasn't sure how I felt about this other young lady. She was certainly brash and vulgar, and I didn't like her calling me Grandpa. Still and all, after having Molly describe her to me, I wanted her. Just as badly as I wanted Molly.

Chapter 5. Angie arrives.

I had been at the store when Angie first arrived that following Monday, and when I saw the beat up old Toyota parked at the side of the house my heart lept with excitement. I grabbed the grocery bag and walked around to the back of the house, looking in the kitchen for signs of Molly's friend but seeing only Ethel.

"Molly's friend is here," Ethel said with a roll of her eyes as I entered the kitchen.

"That's nice," I said casually while putting the milk in the fridge.

"Horrible!" Ethel hissed at me. "No wonder they try to keep her away from Molly. She looks like a vampire."

"Just stuff kids do these days to annoy the old-timers," I told Ethel, and I went upstairs to say hello to our company.

When I reached Molly's room the door was ajar, and so I peeked in. There sitting on the bed, was Angie, Molly's friend, and I had to admit she looked a little scary.

Jet black hair cut so short it was like a crew cut, and a lot of eye makeup that did give her a ghoulish appearance of sorts. Angie was wearing jeans and a green army jacket that gave no hints regarding this incredible body she was suppposed to have. As I was checking her out, Angie looked up and saw me in the doorway.

"Hey Grandpa Ed!" Angie said loudly, and I waved and smiled at the brash young woman.

"Hello Angie," I said softly. "You don't have to call me Grandpa Ed. Ed will do fine."

"I like Grandpa Ed better," Angie announced.

"Isn't she pretty?" Molly asked with a smile.

"Oh yes, very much so," I agreed. "You two have fun now."

I pulled the door closed behind me and headed down to my bedroom, shaking my head at the crazy situation I was in, a situation that got crazier when I felt someone grab me from behind and direct me into the bathroom. Angie.

Angie nudged me into the bathroom and put the hook in the eye to secure the door before leaping into my arms. I could taste the cigarette she must have had earlier as her tongue forced its way into my mouth.

"Like tits grandpa?" Angie asked as she reached down and grabbed my hands, bringing them up the outside of her shirt, where they found a pair of breasts that felt gigantic. I groaned as I hefted them through the fabric, while Angie felt around my trousers.

"Holy shit Grandpa!" Angie said as her hand found my cock, which was rapidly energizing down the inside of my thigh.

Angie pulled me over and sat on the toilet seat before me, unzipping my fly and pulling my cock out, yanking on it violently several times to the sounds of my moans of delight.

"Molly wasn't kidding man, this is one big dick," Angie said before bringing it to her mouth.

I looked down as the head of my cock disappeared inside Angie's mouth, and her lips hungrily slid down the shaft, trying to take it all in. No shy young thing was she, for Angie was obviously an experienced cocksucker, and her fist was churning on the base of my cock while her full lips rode up and down the rest of me.

"Arrrgh!" I groaned while I reached over to the wall for support with one hand, and running my other hand through her short slick hair, and at this rate I was about to cum any second.

Just then a noise came from the door, as an attempt was made to open it followed by the startled voice on the other side. Ethel.

"Oh, I'm sorry!" Ethel exclaimed in shock.

"Uh, sorry Grandma Ethel!" Angie said after taking my cock out of her throat. "Be right out."

Angie reached back and flushed the toilet, and stood up and went over to the sink and washed her hands. I had few options. The little window in the shower would have been an impossible exit even if it wasn't on the second floor. Angie smiled at me as she washed her hands, and shrugged her shoulders.

"Better think fast Grandpa Ed," Angie whispered in my ear, and I did the only thing I could think of doing, which was to hop in the shower and pull the curtain closed behind me. Maybe Ethel had gone downstairs and I could duck out after Angie left. Please.

"Sorry Grandma Ethel," Angie said very loudly for my benefit.

"Oh that's okay dear," Ethel said. "Guess I'm not used to having so many people around to use the facilities."

I held my breath as I heard Ethel close the door behind herself, trying not to make the slightest sound as I heard her fiddling with her clothes before plopping down on the bowl. Could she hear my heart beating? My breathing? Just pee and flee, I prayed as sweat poured down my face.

No such luck, as an explosive eruption came from the other side of the curtain, and Ethel let loose with what sounded like one of the most prolific shits in the history of crapping. Another ear-splitting belch of air followed, and the splashing sounds that followed almost made my explode myself, only in laughter.

I was biting my lip as Ethel continued to let loose with the most vile audio display imaginable. Looking down, my cock was still hanging out, but all thoughts of cumming were long gone, as it had shriveled up from terror. How I wanted to just let my laughter go, and it was only fear that kept me choking it back.

"Rock of Ages..." Ethel began first singing, and then humming, and now I was doubled over, tears joining the sweat rolling down my face. The stench was wafting in and surrounding me, and of course the old crow had neglected to turn on the fan, so now I was holding my nose while biting my lip.

More noises followed, both of air and tinkling, and I was on the verge of passing out. If it had gone on another minute I was thinking of just jumping out of the shower and saying the hell with it. Mercifully, the toilet flushed and Ethel pulled her ass off of the bowl, and went over to wash her hands. A minute later the door opened, and sweet fresh air poured into the bathroom.

I waited a minute before climbing out of the shower and crept to the door, peeking out. All clear. I looked at the mirror at my sweaty, crimson face, and realized that I had dodged another bullet.

Down the hall I went, and as I passed Molly's room I heard the two of them giggling. It was pretty funny, I supposed, depending on which side of the door you happened to be on. Tomorrow night had better be worth it, I thought to myself.

PART VI

Chapter 1. Thinking about the possibilities.

Dinner with the four of us had been a bit of an awkward affair that Monday evening, with Angie's brashness making Ethel cringe on several occasions. This made me chuckle, very quietly of course, because I had a feeling that Angie was being on her best behavior as it was.

The bathroom adventure was still very much on my mind, as I was still quite aroused from the few seconds Angie had been gobbling my pecker. As for those breasts, well let's just say that having felt them through that bulky military shirt, I wanted to see them in the worst way, so I spent the dinner and much of the rest of the evening trying to make them out through Angie's shapeless blouse.

Molly and Angie had retired to Molly's room, where they closed the door behind themselves, leaving them to do... whatever they wanted to do with each other. The image of my little Molly being fondled and groped by this aggressive girl and being forced to submit to whatever deviate acts Angie demanded, made my cock as hard as steel the entire night.

Going off to bed, I slowed at the closed door of Molly's room, listening for whatever was going on in there. The room was dark, I noted as I looked at the space below the bottom of the door. The room was silent as well; no moaning, no groaning and no conversation. What were they doing? My mind worked on the possible scenarios as I went down the

hall.

Chapter 2. "Even a pervert like you..."

I thought I had waited long enough, but my timing must have been off, because when I got to bed Ethel was still awake. I undressed in the darkness as I heard her fretting and tossing in bed, and when I slipped under the sheet, Ethel was ready and waiting.

"Dear Lord! What is tarnation is wrong with that girl's parents?" Ethel declared in an angry hiss.

"Whose parents?" I said in a wear voice.

"That Angela's parents!" Ethel snapped. "Dear Lord, the girl has no manners, no couth! No wonder Molly isn't supposed to be around her. You should have seen the way she paraded in here the afternoon. Even a old pervert like you would have been appalled!"

"What do you mean?" I asked, not needing to feign ignorance this time, because I had no clue as to what the hell she was talking about.

"This Angela - well, the first thing is she's always calling me Grandma. And you Grandpa!"

"Really?" I asked. "Hadn't noticed," I lied.

"And what a sight she was when she came charging in here!" Ethel continued as if I hadn't said anything. "She's a skinny little thing, but all bosom! She was wearing a skimpy little tank top that hardly hid anything, and you could see right through the thing anyway. No shame at all!"

"She seemed dressed okay to me when I got here," I noted.

"That's because I insisted she go put some clothes on!" Ethel said proudly. "I told her that we didn't go around here parading naked in front of each other. Imagine the idea of it!"

"Naked?" I said faux-sleepily, with my erection in full bloom as I envisioned the sight.

"Might as well have been," Ethel snorted. "Never seen bosoms that size on a young girl before in my life, and they were flopping around for all to see. She has tattoos too, on her arms and goodness knows where else."

"You should have asked her about other tattoos," I mused and then got a little brave with the sarcasm. "Maybe tomorrow you can check her for lumps too and find out."

"Don't care much what happens to that little hussy," Ethel said. "It's just that it's not lady-like to go around flaunting yourself like that."

"Let's see... Molly's breasts were too small and this girl's are too big," I commented. "What have you become, Goldilocks or something? They're just kids even if they are eighteen. Let them be."

I was kicking myself for missing Angie's entrance, and was stuck with a raging hard-on and my imagination, as I hoped Ethel would tire of this conversation and go to sleep, which she did eventually, but not before firing off a final salvo.

"Shouldn't go to bingo tomorrow night," Ethel muttered. "I ought to stay home and keep an eye on things around here," Ethel offered. "Goodness knows what you'll allow to go on."

"Suit yourself," I answered, and her veiled threat barely registered with me. Although Ethel staying home would be an unmitigated disaster, it would never happen, because the old biddy would miss my funeral if it happened on a Tuesday night.

Hell, one time there was a fire in the kitchen of the bingo hall and they practically had to drag the murder of crows out of the hall, so desperate were they to hover over their bingo cards no matter what.

Ethel would go to bingo alright, and I would get to see for myself just how disgusting this Angie could be.

Chapter 3. A couple hours later.

The sound of the toilet flushing woke me up, but I had been sleeping so lightly that it could hardly be called sleep at all. I rolled quietly out of bed and exited the bedroom as quietly as I could to attend to business of my own in that room.

As my kidneys did their usual reluctant thing before emptying themselves, I wondered which one of them had been in here a minute earlier, doing a little tinkling of their own. The memory of Molly holding my cock while I went made my loins surge, and so I wrapped it up as fast as I could before flushing.

After doing a quick wash and dry of the hands I opened the bathroom door and headed back to bed. Something made me turn around to the other end of the hall, and when I looked back I saw her.

"Hi Grandpa Ed," the voice whispered.

Half hidden around the corner peeked a face, and the outline of what appeared to be a very naked body. Angie.

"Wanna play with me?" Angie whispered, and then disappeared from view, and I heard her footsteps going down the stairs.

I followed, and when I got down the stairs there she was again, peeking around the kitchen entrance before ducking away. I followed her into the kitchen where I caught sight of her again, now opening the door to the cellar and fumbling for the light before clicking it on.

"You're getting warm Grandpa Ed," Angie teased, and she went down the cellar stairs with me in hot pursuit, the tiny glimpses of her naked backside providing all the incentive necessary.

When I got down to the cellar, which is a typical dirt floor room that was used to store canning goods and produce back in the days when this was an more of an actual farm and I was more of an actual farmer, and now mostly contained odds and ends and junk, I saw her. She would have been hard to miss.

Chapter 4. Breaking my cherry.

Angie stood over to the east side of the cellar, in one of the less cluttered areas of the room, right behind the bare light bulb which provided a limited degree of illumination to that space. Angie was naked, and not only was she making no effort to hide it, she was doing everything she could to display it. And what a display it was.

Angie was holding the beam above her head with both hands, smirking as I walked over to her, and chuckling when she saw my pajamas straining to conceal my erection. She looked less eerie without the ghoulish eye shadow and make-up, but I barely noticed her face.

I stopped about four feet from Angie, frozen in either shock or awe as I took in the view. Angie was a very slender girl indeed, even more so than Molly. I figured I could reach around and encircle her skinny biceps with my thumb and forefinger, noticing that Angie had tattoos of chains around each of those biceps doing that very same thing.

Traveling downward, my eyes took in the sight of the thick tufts of coal black hair that filled the hollows of Angie's armpits, and the sight not only did not revolt me, but instead aroused me even more.

Below that were Angie's pride and joy, those breasts that Molly and Ethel had described already to me, but words could not do them justice. Angie's gigantic breasts stood out like footballs, and their size was accentuated further by the fact that they were attached to such a slender torso. Another thing they didn't make today like they used to was 18 year old girls, I must admit.

I lurched forward as if in a daze, my hands reaching and grabbing for those torpedo-like breasts, and they were as incredibly firm as they looked, and despite their massive size showed not a trace of sagging. Her fat, taut nipples dug into my palms as I hefted the huge globes, and Angie twisted and turned as if she was attached to the beam above her.

"Ooooh Grandpa," Angie groaned. "Like my big tits?"

"Yes," I grunted as I continued to knead them roughly.

"Want to taste something Grandpa?" Angie asked. "Kiss me and see if you can guess what I ate?"

I leaned forward and kissed her on the lips, and her full lips met mine while her tongue dueled with mine, and I inhaled the arousing fragrance that Angie's face reeked of.

"Molly," I said as our kiss ended.

"That's right Grandpa," Angie smirked. "Bet you know what part of Molly it was too, don't you?"

"Her cunt," I said in a zombie-like voice. "Your mouth tastes like Molly's cunt."

"Right you are Grandpa," Angie said. "You did a nice job shaving that little pussy too, Grandpa Ed. Why don't you get those pajamas off so I can see you now."

I pulled my pajama top off me, smashing my hand on the ceiling but feeling no pain, and then stepped out of my pajama bottoms. My erection sprang up and down like a diving board as I stood there naked with Angie.

"Mmmmm... not bad for a old timer," Angie said as her eyes took in the sight of my 61 year old body which, while not bad for my age, was still 61 years old. "That cock is everything Molly said it was. Damn! I like your hairy chest too, Grandpa. Little hair doesn't scare me off. Matter-of-fact, it turns me on. How about you Grandpa? You seem to like it, or do you want to shave me too?"

I saw my hands slide over Angie's breasts like they belonged to someone else, and my fingers slid through the dense, coarse hair under her arms, which caused Angie to let out a little gasp as I did.

My eyes traveled down between Angie's legs, and although it was tough to see in the dim light and shadows, they was no hiding the fact that Angie had a thick and wild bush of hair around her pussy, and my hand found that fur equally dense and coarse to the touch.

"Like 'em hairy, huh Grandpa? Got some around my asshole too. Molly said you never fucked anybody in the ass before, that right?" Angie asked, and I nodded silently.

"I got it ready for you when I heard you go to the can," Angie said. "Glad it was you in there instead of your wife. Can't believe she won't take that beautiful piece of meat in that big ass of hers."

Angie looked around and walked over to an old chair that was covered with junk. Was, was the proper term, because Angie tossed the stuff on the floor and hopped on the dusty old chair, kneeling with her ass in the air and her face in the musty decaying fabric.

"Hard and fast pops," Angie said as I moved behind her and put my hands on her little ass cheeks and spread them further.

Angie had a tattoo of an eagle or something on her lower back, I noticed while sliding my cock around the crack of her ass, feeling it all slick and lubricated, and even in the dim light I could see the hair that grew so abundantly around her pussy extended all the way up to her asshole, which the head of my cock soon found.

"I want it all Grandpa," Angie said before grunting loudly as my crown of my cock entered her.

The shaft of my cock was in my fist and clenched in a death grip as I pushed myself into Angie. After I got the ridge of the head past her relaxed opening, it was a tight but welcoming slide inside Angie's ass, almost all the way in.

"Aw fuck, that's good!" Angie spat out as my cock filled her rectum. "Hard!"

"Keep quiet!" I hissed angrily, because even though we were down in the cellar, I wasn't sure how far the noise would carry in the quiet house.

I began slowly sliding in and out of Angie's ass, and the warmth of her cavity was amazing to me, as was her ability to not only take me into her, but to thrust back at me every time I slid in. My thrusts became harder, and Angie grunted each time I rammed into her.

My hands on Angie's hips, I held her little ass cheeks apart as I humped her, towering over her lithe frame like a praying mantis. I wanted so much to reach down and grab those colossal tits of hers again, but the position I was in was so comfortable and easy to pound into Angie, that I fought the urge and kept pumping.

The cool dirt floor was making the soles of my feet the only part of me not sweating, and sliding my hands up Angie's back found her skin slick as well. Should have put a brighter bulb in down here, I thought to myself, because I would have loved getting a better look at what we were doing.

My balls were swinging wildly as I moved, and Angie's hand reached up from between her legs and grabbed the sack, twisting and pulling my scrotum. I heard Angie start to whimper a little, and her voice was muffled as she came, her ass clamping down on my cock in a series of convulsions.

"Shoot your load in me Grandpa Ed," Angie said in a voice filled with considerably less bravado than earlier.

With my nuts being practically wrung dry by Angie's hand, it was no problem to comply, and I felt Angie's body quiver with each spurt of seed that shot into her ass, my knees buckling with the force of my orgasm.

Standing over Angie with my spent cock still in her, I felt her ass muscles begin to try and squeeze me out of her, and I let her do it, ever so slowly. I pulled myself out and watched Angie get out of what had to be an incredibly awkward and uncomfortable position and get to her feet.

"Mmmm... you like me Grandpa Ed?" Angie said as she reached up and hugged me, those breasts making it none too easy as task. "You liked taking me in the ass, didn't you?"

"Yes," I said.

"Better get some sleep Grandpa Ed," Angie said softly while kissing my neck. "Got a big night ahead of you. I want you to do it to Molly like that too."

"No," I answered. "She doesn't want to."

"She wants to alright, Grandpa," Angie said. "Trust me," she said as I pulled my pajamas back on.

With that, Angie walked around me and headed back up the stairs, with me trudging slowly behind her. Not so slowly that I missed the sight of Angie's backside up the stairs in front of me. Those skinny legs, and that pert little bottom; the one I had just had my cock in, disappeared around the corner and out of sight.

What a difference betwen front and back, I thought to myself as I got up to the kitchen and turned the cellar light off. The sight from the rear was that of a petite teenager, and the front view was that of an incredibly well developed woman.

I went up the stairs with considerably less enthusiasm than I had gone down them, and saw Angie duck into the bathroom when I got up there. I waited down at the end of the hall as Angie did her thing.

The door to Molly's room was ajar, and when I peeked in I saw Molly standing by her bed, naked.

"Hi Grandpa," Molly said in a soft and sad voice, and I felt a rush of guilt as I whispered hello to her. Almost as if I had been cheating on her.

I stepped inside the room and went up to Molly, and she had a brave little smile on her face that was as transparent as could be. I wrapped my arms around her and gave her a hug.

"Remember when we first started messin' around, and I told you about all the boys I did it with and junk like that?" Molly asked me.

"Of course I remember," I assured Molly. "That never bothered me either, if that's what you're concerned about."

"No, that's not it," Molly said. "I lied about it."

"About what, honey?"

"Almost everything," Molly said with fear in her eyes. "I've been with boys - you know, like sucked their dicks and jerked them off and stuff, but I never... did it with any of them."

"You were a virgin?" I gasped incredulously.

"Yes, I lied about doing it with other boys so you wouldn't feel weird about us being together," Molly said. "I always tell Angie those stories so she doesn't think I'm square or anything, but I never did it with any boy before you. I was saving myself for someone special."

"Oh Molly, my baby," I said as I hugged her tightly and my voice choked up.

"Are you mad at me for lying?" Molly asked.

"No Molly, of course not," I assured her. "I could never be mad at you. You've made me come alive since you arrived. Before you came, I was a dead man walking, with no reason for existing. A hollow shell of a man. Now I love life, and even though what we do is wrong, I can't help it. That's how much I love you."

We hugged and kissed for a long time before finally breaking apart, and Molly wiped the tears from her cheeks with the backs of her hands.

"I feel better now Grandpa Ed," Molly said. "We're gonna have a good time, and I'm gonna make you really happy."

"I'll bet you will," I told her as we headed upstairs, and the sound of the shower running meant that we weren't keeping Angie waiting.

"Didn't mean to be a baby downstairs," Molly said. "Guess I'm just insecure, and I know that I'm not much to look at compared to Angie. Hard to believe I'm a month older than her, huh Grandpa? Did you like her boobies? Aren't they something?"

"Yes, she's very shapely," I said. "Remember what I told you last night."

"I know, but she's so well developed - like she's a real woman," Molly said. "Me, I'm just a..."

"Real woman too," I said in finishing her sentence for her. "You're every bit the woman she is, and even more so to me, Molly. Don't be put off over superficial things. Always remember that I'd walk through a herd of Angies to get to you."

Chapter 2. Angie's out of the shower.

A minute after the shower turned off we heard the bathroom door open and Angie padded down the hall and into Molly's bedroom where Molly and I were sitting.

"Thought you two would be naked already," Angie said as she stood in the doorway stark naked and dripping wet, holding a towel in her hand and smiling.

Angie in broad daylight was even more impressive a sight that she had been the night before. Those huge breasts seemed larger than ever, completely commanding your attention, large crimson aureolas capped with thick stubby nipples that were already taut.

"Would you like it if I dried off Angie?" Molly asked me, and I nodded silent agreement as Molly took the towel from Angie and began drying her back.

Angie smiled at me and ran her hands through her short jet black hair, glistening and wet and even more black than seemed possible. Those skinny arms with the tattoed biceps raised high, as if to showcase her brazen animal-like sexuality, and to signal that all was there for the taking.

Molly giggled as she rubbed the towel under Angie's arms, drying and fluffing up the thick tufts of hair that filled the deep crevices with a denseness and a volume which seemed impossible for a woman, or man.

"Angie's got real hairy armpits, doesn't she Grandpa Ed?" Molly said. "Want my Grandpa to shave yours Angie?"

"No, I like mine the way they are," Angie said. "What do you think Grandpa?"

I nodded and swallowed with difficulty, my erection now throbbing in my pants.

"Grandpa shaved mine a couple of times, and it was a lot of fun, wasn't it Grandpa Ed?" Molly declared. "Now I'm letting mine grow again, see Ang?"

"Alright, you go girl!" Angie cackled as Molly lifted her own arms to show her friend the little wisps of fur barely visible even after a few weeks.

Molly went back to drying Angie, working on her breasts with the towel. Angie lifted the huge torpedo-like boobs to allow Molly to dry underneath them, before Molly brought

the towel down and rubbed it through the thick mat of hair that surrounded her pussy.

"Mmmm - that's it babe. That's nice," Angie said as she spread her thighs apart. "Let me get your clothes off now."

Molly raised her arms to allow Angie to pull her blouse over her head, and now Molly was naked to the waist. Angie was a couple of inches taller than Molly, and when they hugged, Angie's massive tits crushed against Molly's little buds.

I had to turn away, because I thought I was about to cum just from watching, and fought back the urge with all my might.

"What's the matter Grandpa?" Molly asked as she looked over at me.

"Nothing honey," I choked out. "You two look very nice together."

"Grandpa wants to get naked too," Angie said as she pulled off Molly's panties, leaving me the only one with a stitch of clothing on. "Let's make him feel comfortable too, okay Molly?"

I stood up as the two girls came over to me, and Angie began unbuttoning my shirt while Molly reached up and kissed my neck. The shirt came off and Angie ran her hands through the thisck coating of grey hair that covered my chest, tweaking the nipples roughly. Molly seemed to be watching Angie and mimicking her actions, so now they were both sucking on my nipples.

"Oooooh!" I moaned reflexively as they bit and and chewed on my nubs, and then a shiver ran all through my body as Angie chewed her way up my shoulder and neck, and even lifted my arm to nibble my armpit, with Molly parroting her actions and my knees almost ready to give out.

Angie dropped to her knees and unbuckled my belt, and my pants fell to the floor, leaving me with my boxers and socks.

"Look at what we did to Grandpa, Molly," Angie said, running her hand over the bulge in my shorts. Shorts that had a massive stain that covered the whole front of them, or so it seemed. "Grandpa looks like he popped a load in his drawers already."

With Molly on one hip and Angie on the other, the snap on my boxers came undone, and the shorts were worked down. My cock came free and sprang around wildly, the vein that ran down the center of the shaft never more prominent, the crown beet red and taut.

"Omigod!" I groaned as I looked down and saw Molly and Angie began licking the sides of the shaft, starting from the shaved base and running along the length of it to the ridge of the crown, before sliding back down to the base.

Again and again they repeated the slow licking, and my cock was jumping and twitching with each slide of their tongues. I put my hands to the tops of their heads, running my hands through their hair as I watched this fantasy come true.

"Look at the cum ooze out of your Grandpa's cock," Angie said. "Let's clean it up."

With that their tongues slid along the crown and met at the tip. I watched as the two girls dabbed and licked at the tender opening of my cock, while dueling with each other's tongues at the same time.

Stringy ropes of cum were stretched off and lapped up by the girls, and more kept oozing out to replace it. Angie's hand went to my balls, milking and kneading the sack as if to coax more out, or to make me cum altogether.

Cum. I wanted to cum, but I also wanted to hold off on that as long as I could, because there were so many things I wanted to do. So many places I wanted to cum. The vein that ran down the top of my shaft seemed to be throbbing as the tongues ran along each side of it.

I grabbed the two teens by the hair and gave a gentle upward tug, and they responded by getting up.

"Can't decide what to do first, can you Grandpa?" Angie said as if reading my mind. "I wnat to watch you fuck Molly with that big thing, and I want you to fuck me too. Molly wants to tell you something too, I think. Unless she's chickened out."

"I haven't chickened out," Molly said defiantly, and then looked over at me with those soft doe-like eyes. "I want you to put your dick in my bottom tonight."

My heart skipped a beat as I looked at Molly, who returned my gaze with a mixture of excitement and fear. That tiny little orifice; so virginal and vulnerable looking, and the object of my dreams for so many nights, was to be mine.

"Later for that," Angie announced, having become the director of sorts. "First I gotta see you two fuck!"

Chapter 3. Angie sets the table.

Angie pushed Molly down on the bed and ran her hand over her smooth mound while she looked back at me.

"Ooooh! She's wet already," Angie said before lowering her face into Molly's tender moist opening and began to lap her loudly.

Molly's face was telling me everything I need to know about how it felt, as her eyes rolled back in her head under Angie's tongue. My hand idly stroked my cock slowly, as if

it needed to be kept any more interested.

"Fuck her!" Angie said as she rolled out from between Molly's legs to make room for me.

I climbed onto the bed and crawled between Molly's soft thighs. Looking down, I saw the smooth glistening mound dripping with Angie's saliva, and as I took the head of my cock and ran it up and down the opening, I heard Angie groan.

Angie was kneeling on the bed next to us with her legs spread wide. Her one hand was squeezing her breast while her other hand was furiously working between her legs, her fingers burrowing into her bush as she watched us.

"In... Put it in!!!" Angie said, and as I slipped the bulbous head of my cock into Molly, along with Molly's gasp I heard Angie wail.

My attention was diverted by Angie's howling, and I watched incredulously as fluid squirted out from around her hand as she frigged herself wildly, her entire body shaking.

I had to turn away so that I didn't lose it myself, but the sight of my little Molly's face contorting as I impaled her sweet pussy was equally arousing, so I closed my eyes while I began slowly stroking myself in and out of Molly.

"Fuck!" Angie said as she regained a bit of her composure. "That looks so fucking hot! How's that feel baby?"

"Big," Molly squeaked as I began to increase the tempo of my thrusts.

"Put it all the way in," Angie said. "Split that pussy in two."

I was working a little more into Molly with every stroke, but didn't want to hurt her, so I kept on going the way that I knew Molly liked it. Angie grabbed Molly's hand and pulled it up between her legs and into her dripping bush.

"You know what I want," Angie said, and Molly apparently did, because the next thing I knew Molly had scrunched up her little hand and was sliding the whole thing in and out of Angie's cunt.

Molly came after a few minutes of this, and after she did, Angie announced that she wanted her turn.

"Give it to me like you did last night, Grandpa. Fast and hard."

Molly rolled over as I extracted myself from her, and helped me put my cock into Angie's pussy. Her pussy was not nearly as tight as Molly's, and as I slid into her, Angie howled.

"All of it Grandpa!" Angie screamed. "I want all of that fat cock in me."

Angie was an attractive and exotic looking girl, but she had a way about her that got on my nerves occassionally, so when she said that to me, I decided to give her what she asked for.

I slammed myself into her all the way in, right down to my nuts. When I felt the head of my cock slam into the back wall of her pussy, Angie let out a scream that was so feral and bloodcurdling that a shiver ran down my spine.

"AAAAAHHHHHH!!!!!" Angie screamed as her entire body lurched backwards, almost slamming her skull into the headboard as it did.

She kept screaming as I rammed myself into her as hard as I could, again and again. My body protested, my back ached and my shoulders made me wince, but I was beyond caring. I thrust into her like a man possessed, with a savageness that surprised all three of us.

Angie came hard, her pussy clenching down on my cock hard as she did, but that didn't stop me from continuing. Sweat was flying off of me as I fucked Angie, while Molly looked at me with a smile and her face and and her hands pinching her little titties.

I wasn't even trying not to cum any longer, but I just couldn't for some reason. Even looking at Molly pinching her nipples, a sight that usually sent me over the edge, did not work. Finally, Angie's upper torso lifted up of the bed like she was possessed, with her face twisted and tortured. Her pussy clamped down on me a couple of times weakly until her shoulders fell back on the bed, eyes rolling back in her head.

"Holy shit," Angie moaned slowly, the defiant and sassy attitude somehow missing from her by this point.

"Want it in your ass now, Angie?" I asked her as I extracted my cock from her.

"Later..." Angie said weakly.

"Me Grandpa," Molly said. "Why don't you get on your back and let me ride you? You look like you could use a rest."

That was the understatement of the year, I thought to myself as I fell onto my back. I was exhausted, and most of all I wanted to cum. Molly climbed over and straddled me, holding my cock gingerly in her hand.

I hardly recognized my trusty weapon, as it was almost purple in color in Molly's pale hand. How long had I been fucking? Time seemed to be something incomprehensible. Molly's clock was blinking 12:00 incessantly, a reminder of the brief power outage of earlier in the day.

Now Molly was sliding down onto my cock, her tight pussy a familiar feel as she slowly rocked her hips to a beat only she could hear. She had about half of me in her as she danced on my tool, smiling down at me as I watched.

"You can cum if you want to," Molly said.

"Man, you have some kind of control," Angie said with a degree of respect in her voice, something I couldn't recognize coming from her.

Fact was that I wanted to cum, but had fought the sensation for so long that I was having trouble getting there. Still hard as a rock though, and as long as it felt good I was not going to complain.

Chapter 4. The grand finale.

Molly rode me for quite a while, and Angie regained a little bit of her bravado and energy by climbing up and straddling my face. Her thick bush surrounded my cheeks as I slid my tongue inside her slightly musty and slippery cunt.

I tongued away at Angie, and after a while I heard Molly start to whimper as she began rocking on my cock harder. Her pussy clenched down on me hard as she came and then I felt her climb off me, followed by Angie.

"I know what will get you off Grandpa," Angie said as she looked at my crimson cock with the purple head so taut it looked ready to burst. "You gotta nail that ass."

I looked at Molly, who was looking at my cock, biting her lower lip. When she looked back at me she nodded tersely.

"You don't have to baby," I said

"She wants it," Angie said, but I wanted to hear it from Molly.

"Yes Grandpa."

"I'll prep her for you," Angie said as she reached over for the bottle of baby oil.

I climbed off the bed as Molly got on all fours, with that pale woman-child body looking so vulnerable and innocent, even more so than normal. Angie squirted some oil in her hand and had Molly spread her cheeks. That puckered pinkish/tan ring was now fully exposed, and Angie wasted no time in penerating the tender opening with her lubricated index finger.

"Ow!" Molly yelped.

"Be gentle," I told Angie, who extracted her digit and then looked over at my throbbing

cock as if to say, if you think I'm hurting her now...

Angie went back to working her finger in and out of Molly's anus, and Molly began to rock in rhythm with the penetration of the digit. Angie looked over at me and winked, and then suddenly pulled her finger out and, spreading Molly's ass cheeks open, buried her face between her buttocks.

"Ooooohhhh!!!" Molly squealed as Angie's tongue burrowed into her ass, her head wiggling around as she licked and thrust around inside her.

"All yours," Angie finally said as she pulled up from Molly, and I nodded as I climbed behind her.

I put the tip of my crown against the opening and made a couple of timid thrusts, making every effort to not hurt Molly. Molly began pushing herself back into me, trying to force it into her.

"I want it Grandpa," Molly said. "Don't worry, it won't hurt bad."

I grabbed the shaft of my cock and pushed hard. The head of my cock worked inside her gradually, and I tried to take the thought of the damage I might be doing to my little princess out of my head.

When the ridge around the head of me finally got inside her ass with a pop, I lurched a little bit forward. Molly was screaming, and it sounded like she was crying and so I pulled myself out of her.

"It's okay Grandpa," Molly whimpered. "Put it back it in!"

I looked back down at Molly's ass and saw that her little puckered opening had become so wide that you could have dropped a golf ball in it. My cock slid back in much easier this time, and soon I was doing it at last. Fucking my granddaughter in the ass.

I kept my fist wrapped around the shaft of my cock so I didn't get carried away. Tight... so impossibly tight Molly's ass was. Hot too. Molly was yelling for me to fuck her harder, and Angie was reaching down and squeezing my nuts, pulling and yanking on them wildly.

It was all a blur the next few minutes, and what I remember is more of a series of images in my head.

Molly was screaming at me, but I don't remember if she was screaming at me to stop or don't stop.

I looked over at the mirror and saw our glistening bodies crashing together, with me crouched over her like a praying mantis ready to devour my prey.

Angie was screaming too, and then she went down behind me to the foot of the bed.

Now Angie's finger was sliding inside MY ass, wiggling around... searching for a special spot which she eventually found.

Molly was cumming - I think. Her ass was like a vice around my cock.

Angie's finger came out, and then I felt my own ass cheeks being spread. Was that her tongue?

I started cumming. I was screaming myself now; my seed blasting into Molly in torrents, my cock like a jackhammer inside of her, Angie tongue doing things unimaginable to me a few moments earlier. My orgasm finally began to ebb after what seemed like an eternity.

Chapter 5. And then...

Then another scream filled the room. A scream of horror, in a voice that I didn't immediately recognize. Following the scream, a loud thump. Both the scream and the thump had come from the hallway.

When I looked back toward the hall a few seconds later, it suddenly occured to me that the party was over. I saw the familiar blue tennis shoes, and the swollen ankles encased in white socks. The rest of Ethel was laying in the hallway, where she had landed, right on top of a whole shit load of money. Fives and tens and twenties.

"This is one crazy fucking house!" I remember Angie saying as we went out to the hall, and for once Angie finally made some sense.

Chapter 6. Aftermath.

Ethel had a stroke, the doctors told me. Her blood pressure had been a problem for quite a time, and it was only a matter of time until it would finally catch up to her.

"Apparently the shock did it," the doctor told me, after I had explained that Ethel had come running home that evening all excited.

"She had won the last game - $500, and she couldn't wait to tell me about it," I said, leaving out the part about what had likely triggered it. What else was I going to say?

"Well doc, the old lady came home early, and I guess I had lost track of time. She comes down the hall, and there we were. My cock had just finished shooting what seemed like a quart of cum into my grandaughter's ass, and her friend Angie was just pulling her tongue out of my own ass..."

No, that wouldn't do.

"She may get a little better, but the likelihood is that she will stay about the way she is," the doctor explained. "She's not in any pain or anything, she's just... well... in her own little world."

"Poor Ethel," I said sadly. "What should I do? How should I treat her?"

"Just make her as comfortable as you can."

"What about sex?" I asked him. "Can we have sex as much as we did before?"

Apparently the doctor didn't catch the dripping sarcasm in my voice, because he assured me that it would be fine, and that Ethel might enjoy it.

"It even might bring back fond memories," he suggested, and I resisted the urge to tell him that her memory wouldn't have been that good even before the stroke.

Angie had flown the coop right after Ethel had hit the ground, all traces of the brashness gone.

Molly had stayed with me for a couple of days after the incident. She was a little shaken but stuck with me bravely as we spent the days at the hospital, sitting with Ethel in her room.

At night we made love like schoolkids, without having to wait for bingo night. It took a couple of days for Ethel's son and his wife to be found, since they were on vacation somewhere in France, and we made the most of it.

By the time Molly's mom and dad came to see Ethel and eventually take Molly back home, I was ready for a break. I was beginning to feel my age, and realized I would never be able to keep up a pace like that much longer before I would end up like Ethel.

After a few weeks Ethel was sent home, and I got to take care of her. I couldn't afford to send her to a nursing home, and besides I did feel guilty about it, so I made the most of it.

Chapter 7. Help arrives.

I decided to hire someone to help take care of Ethel, so that I could get a break from the drudgery of it all. The agency sent over a young woman from a nearby town, and she would come over about six hours a day four or five days a week,

Her name was Gail, and she was a tall, skinny girl with big teeth. She didn't seem too bright either, but at least it was another person to talk to from time to time.

Before then, my only amusement was to walk past Ethel as she sat in her wheelchair, and

to suddenly yell out, "B 9" or N 38". This would make her head lift slightly and a smile would invariably follow.

Gail got more attractive to me with each day. She was homely enough, alright, but there was something about her that appealed to me. That feeling grew when she explained to me that she had just turned 18.

"That's how old my granddaughter is," I told Gail as she cleaned Ethel with a washcloth in bed.

A thought crossed my mind as I watched Gail wipe down Ethel's naked body, and I couldn't believe I was saying what came out of my mouth.

"Say, why don't you wait a minute before you clean her up," I said. "We usually have sex on Tuesday anyway, so why don't I just do it before you waste your time cleaning her."

"You have sex with Mrs. Watson?" Gail said in her dull monotone that only made her sound dumber than she probably was, if that was possible.

"Of course," I proclaimed as I went to the guest room, returning with a bottle of baby oil. "The doctor recommended it."

"Okay then, I'll leave you towo alone then," Gail said.

"No no no!" I said. No need to leave. It's not that romantic or anything. It's more like something I do for her to bring back memories. Matter of fact, I had just finished orgasming when Ethel had her stroke."

"Really?"

"Sure, and as matter of fact Ethel would probably like it if you stayed," I claimed outrageously as I lubricated Ethel's cunt.

"Okay then," Gail said, and promptly sat down on the edge of the bed and wiped Ethel's brow. "I won't look."

"Suit yourself, but I don't mind if you do look," I said, as I dropped my pants and squirted some oil on my cock, which had become fully engorged at the thought of what might actually happen. "Might even make it more interesting for me if you did look, because it's not very exciting to do this. More like an obligation for me."

Gail might not have wanted to look, but when she glanced up and saw my cock swaying in front of me, she got interested in a hurry.

It didn't last long. Ethel stared at me blankly as I slid my cock into her and began thrusting. I stared at Gail all the while I fucked Ethel. And Gail, well she stared at my

cock with her mouth open, from the time I oiled it up until after I pulled it out of Ethel.

"There, that wasn't so bad was it?" I asked Gail as I walked around the bed and headed to the bathroom, with Gail following behind me.

"Want to use this?" Gail said as she handed me the washcloth, her eyes still focused on my now-limp member which swung back and forth as I walked.

"If you'd like to...", I suggested, and to my delight Gail began wiping my cock with the cloth.

"Boy Mr. Watson, you sure got a big pecker on you," Gail said. "Never seen one that big before. My boyfriend's got a little one."

"Well, your boyfriend is a lucky guy to have a pretty girl like you," I said, enjoying the color than came to her cheeks as she ran the cloth under the warm water and resumed cleaning.

"I ain't pretty Mr. Watson," Gail said shyly. "I'm ugly and flat-chested."

"Don't be silly," I told Gail as I brushed her hair back from her face. "You're a real cutie, and as far as being flat-chested..."

My hand slid over to rub the little swelling of her breast through the fabric of her uniform.

"You aren't flat-chested, and besides I love small breasted women," I assured her. "In fact, the sexiest girl I ever met had breasts that were even smaller than yours."

"Really?"

"Does it look like I'm lying?" I asked as I nodded down to the washcloth Gail held; a washcloth that was rubbing a very hard cock.

"Mr. Watson... I don't know about this. What about your wife?"

"She already had hers, and now you can have some too Gail," I said as I led her to the spare bedroom, unbuttoning her uniform as we went. "Just do me a favor honey, and please don't call me Mr. Watson."

"What should I call you?" Gail asked as her uniform came off, revealing her slender body and her barely visible breasts.

"Call me Grandpa," I said with a paternal smile on my face, as I slowly lowered Gail back onto the bed.

THE END

This Is a Work of Fiction *involving an incest theme with consenting adults, and produced for adult entertainment only. If you do not agree with an adult incest theme do not read this story.*

All characters are over 18. All names, characters, places and incidents are used fictitiously. Any resemblance to actual events or locales or persons, living or dead, is entirely coincidental.

You MUST be over 18 years old to read this story. If you are under 18 or do not wish to view adult content, you must exit now. <u>Adults Only</u>.

Share your thoughts with us.
Take a moment to tell us how we're doing. Your feedback really matters.

You can reach us by:
Email: <u>*my777books@yahoo.com*</u>

Search for other titles by **Sophie MacDonald.**

www.ingramcontent.com/pod-product-compliance
Lightning Source LLC
LaVergne TN
LVHW011254200326
834410LV00006B/258